FALLEN DEMON

RITE WORLD: FALLEN ANGEL
BOOK 3

JULIANA HAYGERT

COPYRIGHT

This book is a work of fiction. Names, characters, places, and incidents either are products of the author's imagination or are used fictitiously. Any resemblance to actual persons, living or dead, events, or locales is entirely coincidental.

Copyright © 2024 by Dark Witch Press, LLC

All rights reserved. This book or any portion thereof may not be reproduced or used in any manner whatsoever without the express written permission of the publisher except for the use of brief quotations in a book review.

Manufactured in the United States of America.

First Edition November 2024

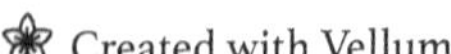

www.JulianaHaygert.com

Edited by H. Danielle Crabtree

Proofread by Kimberly Cannon

Jes Ireland from Black Bird Book Covers

Any trademark, service marks, product names, or names featured are the property of their respective owners, and are used only for reference. There is no implied endorsement if one of these terms is used.

❀ Created with Vellum

AUTHOR'S NOTE

I HOPE YOU ENJOY READING *FALLEN DEMON*!

DON'T FORGET to sign up for my Newsletter to find out about new releases, cover reveals, giveaways, and more!

If you want to see exclusive teasers, help me decide on covers, read excerpts, talk about books, etc, join my reader group on Facebook: Juliana's Club!

RITE WORLD

Welcome to the RITE WORLD!

For a printable reading order, click here!

Free Novellas:
The Vampire Hunt
The Light Witch

Novellas:
The Hunter Path
The Light Calling
The Light Witch
The Wicked Alliance
The Shadow Fae
The Fae Queen

Rite World: Lightgrove Witches
The Midnight Test (Book 1)
The Midnight Spell (Book 2)
The Midnight Flame (Book 3)
The Midnight Secret (Book 4)
The Midnight Hunt (Book 5)
The Midnight Wish (Book 6)

Rite World: Fallen Angel
Dark Wings (Book 1)
Light Magic (Book 2)
Fallen Demon (Book 3)
Wicked Angel (Book 4)

And more to come!

1

I stood in place for a long time, frozen and in complete shock.

This couldn't be happening. No, I hadn't just witnessed Levi and Ylena disappearing in front of my eyes.

"Sweetheart, wish for me to take her to the fiery pits of the underworld."

That was what Levi said. And in that split second, I didn't consider the full extent of his words. I simply thought that with his powers, he would open a portal and send her through.

Not that he would go with her!

I took a step forward, as if I could follow them, and almost fell to the ground as a pang of pain cut through my side. Damn, I had forgotten Ylena clipped me with her magic. I glanced down and saw a red line on my shirt, and it was growing wider and larger by the second.

For half a second, I panicked. What should I do?

Then I kicked myself into gear and moved. I ran back to the motel room, the pain growing more intense with each step. Gritting my teeth, I endured it. I couldn't pass out just yet.

In the room, I found my purse, almost dropped it with my shaking hands, but I found the coins. I closed my hand around one.

Instantly, a portal appeared before me.

I stepped through it.

Into the library in the Great Eternity Hall.

"Ariella?" Abbie asked, coming to me. She grabbed my arms as my knees gave out and I sank to the floor. She crouched down with me. "What happened?"

In a flash, Maggie was beside us. "Where's Levi?"

"He's gone," I rasped, the words thick in my throat.

"What?" Abbie's hand tightened around my forearms. "What do you mean?"

"I—" I gritted my teeth and hissed as the pain went up a few notches.

"She's bleeding!" Maggie yelled.

I turned to her, but dark spots filled my sight. My head swam.

"She's going to—"

The world revolved and I sank into darkness.

***

I woke up with a start, lost and confused.

It took me a moment to remember what happened and where I was—in the infirmary of the Great Eternity Hall. I was lying in one of the beds on the far back, right beside Lacey's bed, though she wasn't there. The sheets were messily folded, as if she had pushed them off her legs and walked away.

Was she better?

She probably was, but not her brother.

My heart squeezed at the thought of him. He had come for me. He had known I was in danger and came for me. He wanted to protect me. And I had sent him to hell.

A sob made its way up my throat, but I swallowed it. I wouldn't cry. No, instead, I would do something about it.

I reached for the side table to grab my phone, an automatic movement, but stopped halfway when I remembered, I didn't have it with me. To my surprise, my bag was on a chair beside the bed. The girls must have gone back through the portal and gotten it after I passed out.

I pulled the bag, picked up the phone from the outer pocket, and glanced at the time. It was midmorning already!

I swung my legs to the side, determined to leave this bed, but groaned when my side pulled.

"It'll hurt for a few more days, but I healed it. You'll be fine."

I snapped my had back. "Lacey." She walked toward me, carrying a tray with food. "You're okay."

She nodded as she set the tray on the nightstand between our beds. "Abbie accessed my healing magic and did a great job."

I remembered that, but I hadn't seen her awake before I left. "I'm sorry about that. You went there for me and—"

"Stop it," she tried snapping at me, but it came out forced. She was too sweet for that. "I wanted to help you." She leaned on her bed. "Though, I heard someone else wanted to help you while I was out and ..." She swallowed hard. "Abbie told me you said my brother is gone. What do you mean?"

"By the light," I murmured.

After taking a deep breath, I told her everything— how I

left without saying goodbye, Abbie opening a portal for me to Boston, me calling Queen Thea at DuMoir Castle to see if the angel Zadkiel could train with me for a couple of days, going to a garage to borrow a car, being attacked by supernaturals who wanted the bounty on my head, being joined by my mentor, Archangel Ylena, who had fled from Elysium after Rhodes tried to sway her to his side—or so she wanted me to believe.

I continued, telling her about canceling my trip to DuMoir Castle, going to an inn with Ylena, training with her, Ylena talking about the Scarlet Hex Dagger ... and me agreeing to go find it soon. Then Levi called me in the middle of the night, saying Maggie had had a vision and I was in danger. I opened up a portal to let him come to me, because he was freaking out, and that was when I learned Ylena was his mother and she was the one actually behind everything. She had ordered Rhodes and Molraz to kill us, but when I escaped, she lied and made it seem like I had lost it and killed them all myself. She had sent angels after me, and when they couldn't find me, she put a bounty on my head.

And then she tried tricking me, pretending she was against Rhodes, so I would lower my guard and give her the damn dagger, because from what she told me, she needed the dagger to kill Adona and create a new Elysium.

But Levi saved me by sacrificing himself.

"When he asked for me to wish him to take her to the underworld, I didn't think that was what he meant," I said, my voice breaking.

Lacey walked up to me and embraced me. I stiffened for a brief moment, then I hugged her back. He was her brother; she should be mad at me.

"He knew what he was doing," she whispered.

"I know, but it doesn't make sense."

She pulled back, a small smile in her lips. "Why not? Wouldn't you die for someone you love?"

My eyes widened, my throat went dry. I shook my head once. "He doesn't care for me. Everything we feel, it's the bond. He did it because of the bond."

"If you say so." She retreated to her bed again.

I wouldn't dwell on what she was implying. It was too much for my head and my heart right now.

"Did you know about his mother?" I couldn't quiet grasp that information, to be honest.

"No, I had no idea."

"My own mentor," I whispered. The archangel I had looked up to, who I wanted to be like. It still felt surreal. Maybe it always would.

"I'm sorry."

I frowned. "Why?"

"This can't be easy for you, either."

I nodded. That was true. I inhaled deeply. "It isn't, but I won't just sit back and wallow in pain. I have to do something about it."

Under Lacey's protests that I had to rest a little—if that was the case, then she had to rest too!—I picked up the food tray and marched to the library.

Abbie and Maggie were hunched over large leather books spread out on the long tables, while the younger siblings were upstairs, studying.

The sisters saw me coming, and Abbie frowned. "What do you think you're doing?"

"I tried stopping her, but she's stubborn," Lacey said from behind me.

I deposited the tray on a corner of the tables, away from all the books. "We have work to do."

I took a chair and munched on my food while I retold the entire tale of what had happened to Abbie and Maggie. When I was done, the tray magically disappeared, like it usually did at the dining room.

"I sent them to the fiery pits of the underworld," I said, my chest hurting with that truth. "Do you know what that means? Is there a chance he could—" I sucked in a sharp breath, afraid of saying it.

"That he could be alive?" Maggie finished for me. "Fiery pits could mean so many things. If he went literally to fiery pits, I'm not sure he could have survived."

"Maggie," Abbie snapped in a hush.

"What?" She stared at me. "Would you rather I lied to you so it would hurt less?"

Maybe? I shook my head. "No. I want the truth. Always."

"Is there a way for us to narrow down what the fiery pits could mean, then?" Lacey asked. "If we can, then maybe we can determine if he's alive or not."

"I think there's a way to know if he's alive or not." Abbie walked up to me and gestured for me to stand. I pushed to my feet. She placed her hand on the center of my chest, right above my breasts, closed her eyes, and inhaled deeply. Her magic tingled as it invaded me, gentle and warm. "The bond is still intact." She opened her eyes. "I'm not one hundred percent, but if I had to bet, that means he's alive."

I sighed in relief. Lacey smiled at me.

"Then, he's somewhere in the underworld," I said with renewed energy. "That means he can just walk out, right?"

"Maybe," Maggie said. "Again, it all depends on where

exactly he and Ylena went. They might be trapped deep in the underworld with no way of leaving."

"Then we need to go after him," I said. "We need to find out exactly where he is."

Abbie looked at the giant bookshelves around us. "There are hundreds of books about the underworld here, and I guarantee you, the information we have won't be complete."

"What do you mean?" Lacey asked. It was the same thing I wanted to know.

"The underworld is a world in itself, as large as the human realm ... or Earth, if not larger," Abbie said. "No one knows the true extent of that place, since it was never fully explored."

Maggie nodded. "I remember mother telling us about it during a lesson. She said it was never fully explored because it was so large. No one had time to map it all, not while there were evil things to be done, humans to terrorize, battles to fight, and whatever else demons and evil beings do."

"So, you're saying there's no way of knowing where Levi is?"

"Only if we're lucky and he went to a place we have records of," Abbie said. "Otherwise, it's like he's lost in a different world."

I sat down on the chair, the hope and excitement deflating. "Wait," I almost jumped up to my feet again. "The bond. We can follow the bond, right?"

"Maybe." Abbie looked at me. "But I doubt it. If you go to the underworld but you're not close to where he is, the bond will take you nowhere. Think as if you were in the United States and Levi was in Australia. The bond wouldn't be able to guide you to him."

I reached for a book, running my fingertips over the

spine. "There has to be something we can do. What if we research the books you have about the underworld, make a list of all the places he could be, and go from there?"

"You're thinking about what?" Maggie asked. "Going to all these places to try finding him?"

I shrugged. "Any better idea? What about a vision? That would help." She flinched and I felt the urge to slap my mouth. "Sorry. I didn't mean it like that."

"I know," she said with a sigh.

"Unfortunately, Maggie's visions don't work at will," Abbie said.

"Yet." Maggie lifted a finger. "I remember reading something in one of mother's diaries about forcing a vision. I bet her older diaries will have more information on it."

"There are dozens of diaries," Abbie said. "It'll take a long time to get through them all."

"I can skim for something about visions." Maggie smiled. "I'll get started!" She skipped off to the library.

"Oh-kay," I said, confused.

"She loves reading those diaries," Abbie explained. "It's her way of getting closer to our mother."

I nodded, understanding that. With a deep inhale, I stood from the chair. "Should we start, then?"

Abbie lifted a finger. "Let's say we gather all the books about the underworld, we make an extensive list of places where Levi could be, and then we go to these places to find him. Do you think we'll waltz into the underworld and waltz out? There will be dangers in every corner, and your magic is still a mess. What are you going to fight with?"

"Well, my plans to train went down the drain," I said, harsher than I wanted.

"I strongly suggest you leave the researching to Maggie,

Lacey, and me," Abbie said. "I'll even ask Gwen and Britt to help to go faster, but you should go to DuMoir Castle. When we find something, we'll come for you."

I opened my mouth to protest, but Lacey had the same determined expression as Abbie.

A list of arguments formed in my head, but I could also see their point. What if we ran into a horde of demons and had to fight? My messy magic could be what put us in danger, hurt Lacey again, or someone else, and I couldn't have that on my conscience.

I groaned. "Fine."

2

THIS TIME, INSTEAD OF ASKING ABBIE TO OPEN A PORTAL FOR ME to Boston, I called Queen Thea. She and Abbie talked about it and agreed that they could do something together.

So, the next morning, after we had breakfast together with the entire family, Abbie and Thea connected through some witchy magic, and Abbie was able to open a portal right at DuMoir's front steps, even though she had never been there before.

"Next time, I'll be able to do it by myself," Abbie said before hugging me and going back to the Grand Eternity Hall.

I should have known Thea wouldn't be the only one waiting for me. Standing beside her in front of the castle's open doors were Prince Killian and Lavinia—I first met the happy, mated couple when they rescued me from some warlocks who were intent on putting me into a magical box and syphoning my powers.

After that, we met again while helping Shane and Raika

defeat the higher demon Paimon and reclaim the Nightshade pack.

They had quickly become my friends.

And several months ago, I left the Nightshade without a word.

"Ariella, welcome back to DuMoir Castle," Thea said, giving me a warm hug.

When I turned to Lavinia, she punched my shoulder. "Do you have any idea how worried we were about you?"

"Sorry," I muttered.

"Are you okay?" Killian asked.

I nodded as I glanced at them. They seemed so beautiful and happy together, it almost made me want to run again. Killian was a handsome vampire prince, and Lavinia was a half witch, half demon hunter, who had turned into a vampire not long ago. They had met when Lavinia accidentally released Killian from a box—the same kind the warlocks wanted to put me in.

"I will be," I said, almost automatically.

Thea took my arm and tugged me forward. "Come on in."

We walked into the castle and I couldn't help but glance around in wonder, though I had been here a handful of times before. The foyer alone was as large as Levi's entire apartment, and I gawked at the smooth floors, the fascinating chandelier, the grandiose stone staircase, and the three-story ceiling.

"Are you hungry? Do you need anything?" Thea asked, guiding me farther into the castle.

I shook my head. "I just need Zadkiel."

"I'm afraid he's still away," she said. "But he sent word early this morning. He should be here in a couple of days."

For those couple of days, what would I do?

"Don't worry, I can train with you until he comes," Lavinia said. "It won't be the same, but we can start with simple spells."

Witch magic and angel magic were like water and oil, but it was probably better than staying seated in a room, waiting for time to pass.

"Sounds like a plan," I said.

"For now, do you want to rest?" Thea asked. "I asked your previous room to be prepared. It should be all ready for you."

A soft smile adorned my lips. I had a room in the famous DuMoir Castle. It was heartwarming.

"I'm fine, no need to rest, but I think we should talk to Drake," I said. Drake was the lord of DuMoir Castle, sort of the king of the vampires, and also probably the most badass supernatural I knew. He and DuMoir Castle oversaw everything that happened in the supernatural world on this side of the globe and interfered if necessary.

Of course, they didn't know about *everything* that went on, but what they knew? They fixed.

Thea nodded. "He wanted to talk to you too, but suggested we gave you some time to rest first. But if you don't want to rest …"

"I'm fine. If he's free, we can go to him now."

We turned toward Drake's office on the second floor.

At the stairs, Thea glanced up and smiled. "Sweetheart, shouldn't you be in class?"

I almost flinched when she said sweetheart, the word causing a slight pain to fill my chest.

I followed the queen's gaze and saw little Aurora standing at the second-floor landing. That kid always took my breath away. Her parents, Drake and Thea, were beautiful and she managed to get the best features of each and mix them together, creating the most stunning person I had ever seen.

In a way, she reminded me of Snow White: white porcelain skin, puckered red lips, bright green eyes adorned by dark lashes, and luscious black hair with coils at the ends.

Sometimes, when looking at her, I forgot she was a little kid. Eight years old now, if I was not mistaken. In a few more years, she would be breaking hearts across the globe.

She would also be one of the most powerful supernaturals ever—half vampire, half witch, Aurora was destined to become the Queen of All Witches.

"I should, but I wanted to see Ariella." Aurora turned to me, her eyes seeing into my soul. "Are you okay?"

I offered her a soft smile. "I am."

"Are you sure?"

I reached the landing and stopped right in front of her. The top of her head hit my chest. "I think so. Why?"

She frowned. "I had a dream about you last night. You were enveloped by shadows, and you fought against it, but your light magic wasn't working."

"Well, I am having trouble with my magic. That's why I'm here."

"I know, but in my dream, the shadows pressed against you, until they were inside of you. Slowly, they filled you completely and they drained you of everything. Magic, blood, energy, life. You became ashes and were taken by the wind into the darkness."

I stared at the girl, shocked. Was this some kind of vision? Did she have that kind of magic?

"It was just a bad dream, sweetie." Thea put an arm around Aurora's shoulders and looked at me. "She overheard us last night when we were talking about your magic. Her dreams … they can be quite vivid."

"But no premonitions related to them, right?" Lavinia added quickly.

"Right." Thea nodded. "None of her dreams have come true."

Yet.

I shook my head. No, I wouldn't go down that rabbit hole. I reached for Aurora and twisted one of her soft curls around my finger. "I'm okay. My magic will be okay. But I appreciate the concern." It meant she cared, right? Such a kind, unique child.

"There you are," a voice came from my left. A witch I had seen before, but didn't remember her name, ran down the hallway. "I was looking all over for you." She glanced at Thea. "I'm so sorry, my queen. I told her to keep reading the book while I gathered supplies. When I came back to her room, she was gone."

"I wanted to see Ariella," Aurora said.

"You should have told Sally where you were going," Thea said. "Anyway, now you've seen Ariella. It's time to go back to your studies. I'll see you later for lunch, okay?"

Aurora nodded, hugged my waist for two seconds, then bounced away, Sally trying to keep up without running again.

I frowned as I watched both of them disappear behind a corner. "May I ask why Aurora isn't in your school?"

Queen Thea had just opened the Silver Moon Academy not far from here.

"Well … two reasons, really. One, there are no kids her age at the school yet. We only have teenagers for now. And … she's already a lot more powerful than all of them. Drake and I agreed it would be detrimental for her and for the other witches if she attended their classes." She let out a sigh. "So, she has been having lessons here."

"It makes sense," I said in a faint voice.

Aurora wouldn't gain anything being among older girls who would probably feel threatened by a child half their age who was more powerful than they would ever be.

But I still felt for the little girl. Being so powerful, so different, and practically isolated because of it, couldn't be good for her.

We resumed our trek to Drake's office.

"Welcome back, Ariella," the lord of DuMoir Castle said when I walked in. He stood from behind his desk and it was hard not to be impressed by him—Drake was tall, strong, lean, with the face of a god, and perfect composure. He looked dashing in a black suit and burgundy tie. The silver cross brooch, the symbol of DuMoir Castle, was pinned to the suit's lapel. "It's good to see you well."

"Thank you," I said. "It'll be better when I get a hold of my magic again."

He nodded once. "I heard about that. Once Zad gets back, you two will work on it."

"That's the plan." I let out a long breath. "But, in the meantime, I should probably tell you what's going on, including why I'm on the run and why Elysium has a bounty on my head."

"If you think that's a good idea, we would love to hear it." Drake gestured to one of the chairs across from his desk.

Thea sat down beside me, while Killian and Lavinia stood behind us, leaning on one of the bookshelves.

I told them all about it. The only parts I left out were about sleeping with Levi, but I thought everyone in this room was smart enough to deduce that.

"All right." Drake leaned back on his chair. "So, you're saying Elysium is about to have a civil war."

I nodded. "That's what I gathered. Ylena wanted the Scarlet Hex Dagger to kill Adona, but I doubt she would have everyone's approval. A group that opposes that is certain to rise and fight them, but Ylena would be ready for that. Now that she's gone, I believe Rhodes will continue with their plans."

"And they still need the dagger?"

"I'm not sure. To kill Adona, yes. To imprison her and take over, maybe not?"

"Either way, Elysium is about to explode and not in a good way," Drake said. "That's not good. Even if the war was contained to your realm, killing Adona, creating new rules, and exploiting and abusing humans? That would create chaos in any realm."

"I wanted to leave you all out of this," I confessed. "But that was back when I thought their issue was with me only, specifically, and I could somehow fix it." Yeah, because wandering Earth alone for five years was a good prognosis of that. "This situation is much bigger than I first realized, and it'll have repercussions everywhere."

Drake nodded. "You know we're here for you and everyone who needs our help."

"We should call on our friends," Thea said. "Have a meeting with them and see who wants to join us."

I sucked in a sharp breath, my chest constricting. If only I had opened up to them earlier, maybe this mess wouldn't be this big, this dangerous. I always knew they had my back. Then why did I resist it?

Because I was a young, stubborn, lost, and proud angel,

who thought she was better than all of these supernaturals. That was why.

But I wasn't better than anyone. Angels weren't better than anyone. There were bad and good angels, just like there were bad and good vampires, witches, wolf shifters and even demons.

Maybe we should introduce new rules to Elysium, but it would be about inclusion, love, friendship, and acceptance.

"I think that's a good idea," I said, my voice showing the emotion twirling within me.

Lavinia put her hand on my shoulder, and Thea reached out, grabbing my hand in hers.

I wasn't alone.

I never was, and never would be again.

3

THE REST OF THE DAY, I DIDN'T DO MUCH.

Thea escorted me to my bedroom.

"In case you forgot where it is," she joked. "This is your home." That wasn't joking, and it once again made me feel stupid and emotional.

That afternoon, I texted Erin and told her to cancel that meeting with the archangels altogether. I bet that by now, she had gotten Drake's message and could add two and two.

After that, I called Abbie—she had no news for me. I took a short nap and when I was bored, I walked around the gardens outside. Lavinia joined me for a little while.

I heard Thea had gone to the school for a couple of hours, and I made a mental note to ask to go with her the next time. I had seen that place only once, when it was still under renovations and construction, and it had already looked amazing. I bet that now, it was breathtaking.

At night, we all had dinner together, including the rest of the castle's princes and new princess! Lyra had proved herself and had become the first vampire princess of DuMoir Castle.

"Congratulations," I told her, feeling proud of her, even though we weren't close.

She had found her mate, Prince Ward of the Red Dusk coven—a rare occurrence for vampires, but always welcomed.

During dinner, Drake told me he had sent a message to our friends, and they would all be here in two days. We would have a meeting and after we would have dinner.

It sounded more social and friendly than I expected a meeting to go, but whatever. These supernaturals were fancy, extravagant, and filthy rich. I guess they expected parties with everything.

I ended up more tired than I thought, went to bed early, and slept like a rock.

Until about five in the morning when I dreamed about Levi burning into a huge fire and screaming in pain.

I woke up with a jolt, my heart racing, my skin covered with a sheen of sweat.

Taking advantage of the suite that comprised the guest bedrooms in the castle, I prepared the Jacuzzi and relaxed in the hot water for about an hour.

Or tried to. Though I stayed in the water for that long, I felt tense and restless. Just sitting around, waiting for things to happen, made me anxious.

After the bath, I got dressed in training clothes I found in my closet. It was full of all kinds of clothes exactly in my size. I had to ask Thea or Drake how they did that. Maybe it was a spell? It had to be.

When I got out the closet, I came to a stop when I saw the tray with breakfast on the round table on one side of the room. Apparently the cook, Chef Morris, remembered what I liked, and one of the maids had come in here while I was in the bathroom.

Creepy.

While eating, I texted Abbie. I knew she wouldn't have anything for me yet, but I needed to do something.

I had just finished my breakfast when my phone dinged with new message.

Lavinia: *Zad arrived a couple of hours ago. He is going to sleep through the morning, and you guys can start training this afternoon.*

I sank into the chair. What the hell would I do until then?

I perked up.

Me: *Okay. I'll be in the library.*

I should have known Lavinia and Killian wouldn't read my message and leave it at that. Shortly after I arrived in the library, they walked in.

"What are we looking for?" Lavinia asked. She wore a dark green gown, making her look like a princess.

Beside her, Killian wore a black suit and burgundy tie, like all the other princes in the castle.

I felt oddly out of place in my tight leggings, vest, and combat boots.

"Any books about the underworld," I said, pushing those thoughts away. How I dressed wasn't important. "I need to find out what fiery pits could mean."

I knew no library would ever match the one at the Great Eternity Hall, but I needed to keep busy. And who knew? I might find something useful in these books.

"We'll help you," Killian said. He grabbed a laptop from the long desk at the front and opened it up. "For the last few years, we've had some lower-ranked vampires enter all the books in the library in a database. They haven't finished it yet. There are so many books and there are always new ones, but I bet we can find most of them here." He took a chair at a squared table.

"Oh, nice." I sat across from him and Lavinia took the chair to his right.

In no time, we had a list of over fifty books. We each took a third of the list and fanned out to grab what we could carry, bringing the volumes to the tables at the front of the library.

After a few minutes of searching, I glanced at my friends. "Are you sure you two don't have something else to do?"

Lavinia lifted an eyebrow. "Why? Want to get rid of us?"

"I just don't want you to waste your time babysitting me."

"We're not babysitting you," she said. "We're helping our friend."

"That's our mission," Killian said.

My lips tugged up, but before they could stretch too wide, I buried my nose in a book and started working. For about one hour, we skimmed through the books, determining the ones that actually talked about the underworld, not just mentioned it as an afterthought, and also the ones that talked about its structure and space.

The next hour, we choose five or six books from the remaining pile and started making a list of common features we found in them. I thought that we would quickly end up with a lengthy list, granted how big everyone kept saying the underworld was, but it turned out, every book said something different about it.

One mentioned how the underworld was its own realm, accessible only by portals, and how it was so large, we would never be able to explore it all.

Another mentioned how the underworld had several levels, like a tall building, and no one knew how exactly each level was reached. By ranking? By power? By portals? And what granted entrance to each level? It was all a mystery.

A third book said the underworld was fluid and kept changing. Good-hearted supernaturals saw more of it, had more access to unusual places; bad supernaturals only saw a prison. But even then, two different good-hearted supernaturals would see different places. Only a limited number of places were the same for everyone.

"This is crazy," I whispered, closing the eleventh book that mentioned only those who died could reach the fiery pits.

And even that wasn't unanimous—so far, some books suggested the fiery pits were a myth, while others said it was a prison, or the real heaven, where dead souls went to rest.

"You're not giving up, right?" Lavinia asked as she turned the page of the giant tome she was studying. "It's too soon."

"Not giving up, but I need a break." A break and a drink. No, it was too damn early for that, but I could use some water. "I'll go to the kitchen and—"

A young page entered the library, his head low. I remembered when I first saw one of these teenagers, I was worried they were slaves, but Drake assured me that there were no slaves.

The teenagers who worked in the castle were either children of the old slaves who didn't want to leave, or orphans they found and offered a new life. They were humans sworn in secrecy about our world, and one day, when older and deserving, they would be given a choice to join us by becoming vampires and entering the official ranking of DuMoir Castle.

"Miss Ariella, Chef Morris sent me to ask what you would like for lunch," the young man said, looking at my feet.

I glanced at the time. It was almost noon. "Hm, I don't know. Why ask me?" Wasn't he cooking for most of the non-vampires in the castle.

"He said you're the special guest of the day and you get to decide the menu," the page said.

Oh, I liked that. "All right, how about one of his famous lasagnas?"

The page nodded and left the library.

"His lasagnas are really good," Lavinia said. "Shame they don't taste the same anymore."

Since she had become a vampire, her taste buds had changed.

All right, I could do this until noon. With a sigh, I grabbed another book and continued researching.

***

THE HOURS STRETCHED AS if they were years, and I was going out of my mind. I tried focusing on the words I was reading, but nothing stuck to mind. Lavinia and Killian tried entertaining me by taking me to lunch—which had been delicious—then a walk around the castle's maze, but all I wanted was to have Zadkiel help me get a hold of my magic and find Levi and kick Rhodes's ass.

In the middle of the afternoon, Zadkiel and Elisa entered the library.

I shot to my feet and my chair almost fell backward.

I had first met Zadkiel in New Orleans, when I was contacted by Norah and asked to help an angel. I took him to the Midnight Cauldron, where he met Khalisa.

Then, we met again while fighting with our friends against Paimon. That was when I asked him about Elysium and what was going on there, but he didn't know anything. After staying for so long in the underworld, Zadkiel had gone back to Elysium, talked to his mentor, Archangel Muriel, and she had sent him back to Earth to stay with Elisa and help the supernaturals at DuMoir Castle.

As far as I knew, Muriel wasn't involved with Ylena and Rhodes, and she probably didn't know anything. I had subtly asked if he had heard about the stories involving me, and he said no, but it was probably because he hadn't stayed up there long enough.

Since then, he didn't have much contact with Elysium, and from what Lavinia had told me, ever since the bounty on my head was announced, his mentor had been quiet. The only thing she had told him was to stay put and continue working for Lord Drake.

"Hi there, Ariella," Elisa said, always the diplomat. She was Queen Thea's right hand and a powerful witch. "It's so good to see you." She walked up to me and gave me a brief but strong hug.

"You too," I said.

"I hear you've been looking for me," Zadkiel said. He was the perfect angel: with longish blond hair, blue eyes, and a serene aura to him. Though, like me, his wings were black.

"Yes." I quickly explained that I had gotten my magic back, but it hadn't been the same. "I need to train to get it under control." Before I bought myself a fight with some demons in the underworld or some angels in Elysium. "And I thought you could train with me."

He probably had already heard all of this from Drake and Thea, as I assumed he already knew everything else I had told them, including what was going on in Elysium.

He nodded. "Of course. Why don't we go to the training grounds and see what we can do?"

I perked up. "Now? Sure."

Waving goodbye to Lavinia and Killian, I followed Zadkiel and Elisa out. I hoped the vampires didn't feel like they should continue working without me and took a break from research.

"I need to go talk to Thea again," Elisa said. She leaned into Zadkiel and I averted my eyes as the two kissed. "You two have fun."

She turned on her heels and disappeared down the stairs.

Zadkiel turned to me. "Are you ready?"

4

DURING THE BATTLE OF DUMOIR CASTLE WHEN LORD DRAKE took over leadership, the original training grounds had burned down. They built new ones, which connected to the castle via an underground tunnel or the garden. We arrived at the gymnasium hidden among the trees. From the outside, it looked like a one-story building, with lots of windows, but once we got in, the place was immense. The first floor rose easily four floors high, and then there were the two underground levels with more rooms and equipment than any human or supernatural could ever need.

Which was ironic since vampires and most supernaturals were incredibly fast and strong naturally. I doubted I would ever see a vampire lifting weights.

The place was almost empty, except for a couple of human servants who were running on the track lining the perimeter of the place.

We paused just past the doors and I watched for a moment.

"Will they be turned?" I asked in a faint voice.

"Eventually, if they continue to be loyal," the angel said.

I knew most humans who lived in the castle wanted to be here and become vampires, and even though I was friends with some pretty cool vampires, I couldn't imagine a human wanting to be one.

"Doesn't that bother you?"

"It used to," Zad said. "But after living in DuMoir Castle for a while, I know turning means salvation for most of these humans."

That made sense.

On the way here, Zadkiel and I talked about Elysium, Ylena, and Rhodes. He said he was shocked by the news. He also told me he hadn't talked much to his mentor lately, and when he tried, she kept the conversations brief.

"That's not like Muriel," he told me. "It feels like she's hiding something from me."

My mentor had been hiding something huge from me, so I couldn't blame him for thinking that.

Zadkiel grabbed what looked like a small remote control from a hook on the wall beside the entrance, then we stopped in the center of the big mat.

"First things first," he started. "Let's see what you can do."

"Not much, considering I can't control it."

He pressed a button on the remote and thin targets in the shape of a person emerged from the end of the mat side by side. "Show me."

I took a few steps back, closed my eyes, and called my magic. It flickered to life inside me, as if annoyed I was bothering it. I gritted my teeth, grabbed a hold of it, and forced it to obey me. The magic surged to my fingertips, fast and fierce, and I threw a light bolt at the target in the center.

The bolt zoomed to it, flickering a couple of times on the

way. It hit the target right in the chest, making it bounce back and forth a couple of times. But the cool part was that when the magic hit it, there was an explosion and it burned, but the target shimmered and was suddenly intact again.

"Enchanted targets," Zadkiel explained when he noticed me frowning at them. "It takes a lot to actually damage them." That was an amazing tool. The angel looked at me. "That wasn't so bad. With your magic, I mean."

"I know, but just ..." I shook my head once and did it again.

This time, it took longer for me to command the magic to my hand and throw it, and it sizzled out before it hit the target. The next one grew as it zoomed to the target, and the explosion should have broken the thing to pieces, if it wasn't enchanted. The next two were like the second, dying before reaching the target, until the bolt barely formed in my palm, and it took a lot of my energy to just try to control it.

All the while, Zadkiel watched me, arms crossed, his brow furrowed.

Breathing hard, I threw my hands out and nothing came out. Frustrated and already tired, I turned to Zadkiel.

"That's what happens. In the middle of a fight, I can't count on my magic." Or worse, I could end up hurting one of our allies. My friends.

"Your magic is there, but it doesn't want to obey you," he said, contemplating. "Usually, our magic is an extension of ourselves. We don't need to think or order it around. It just does what we want it to."

I nodded. "It's strange."

"Very." He uncrossed his arms. "I'm no expert on this, and I haven't trained novices in many years, but I think that's where we have to start. We should pretend you just got your powers and are learning to use them."

I didn't like that, but was there another option? "Sounds like a plan."

FOR THE NEXT THREE HOURS, Zad and I trained as if I was a child learning about her magic. And even though I was doing better than most kids, my magic was as fickle and unstable as before. For extended periods of time, I couldn't even grasp it.

Sweating and breathing hard, I sat down on a bench outside the mat area and drank a big swallow of water—Zad had texted a page and asked him to bring some to us. There were water fountains here, and I had already refilled my water bottle twice.

"I know you're not where you want to be," Zad sat down beside me, "but I think we should stop for the day."

I opened my mouth to complain, but I knew what he meant. I had overexerted myself, and I was frustrated. If I kept going, I would do more harm than good.

Besides, it was getting late and I was so damn hungry.

"Just one more time," I said. I knew one more time wouldn't change anything, but I just had to do it.

Zad nodded in agreement.

I went back to my previous position, stared at the center target as if it was Rhodes, and called my magic. It fought against me, but I grasped it as strongly as I could, and threw a bolt of flickering light magic at the target.

The bolt sputtered and clambered like a car on its last drop of gas. It shook, losing its path, hit the side of the target, and zoomed toward the entrance.

Right when someone was walking in.

A sudden wall of ice appeared before the person. My magic hit the ice with a sizzling sound and melted away.

The wall of ice became snowflakes and disappeared and I stared at the female standing behind it.

"I haven't seen you in a while and the first thing you do is attack me?" Farrah asked, teasing. "What did I do to deserve that?"

She offered a huge smile and walked to me.

I met her halfway. We crashed into each other's arms, hugging as if we would never let each other go.

Farrah was my first friend on Earth, my first supernatural ally. When we first met, I had hated her mate, Wyatt, the wolf shifter, but that was several years ago, when my views were tainted and I thought all supernaturals, except for angels and fae, were dark and evil.

"Don't ever run away without a proper goodbye," she said, still holding me in a bear hug. "Or I'll hunt you down and kick your ass."

I smiled. "Yeah, right now, you might be able to. But if I had my full powers, I'd give you a run for your money."

She pulled back a little and fixed her blue eyes on mine. "How are you?"

I stared at the pretty frost fae. She had long, silver-white hair, brilliant blue eyes, fair skin, and the most delicate, beautiful face I had ever seen. And she was damn powerful.

All of my friends were.

"I'm ... okay."

She squeezed my arms. "Don't lie to me."

Zad cleared his throat. "I'll see you two later."

I gave him a quick glance. "Thanks, Zad."

He nodded once, waved at Farrah, and left the training facility.

"Come." Farrah hooked her arm to mine. "Walk with me."

I did, but when we got outside, I looked around. "Where's Wyatt?"

"He went to help Drake with something." She shrugged. "Preparing for tomorrow night, I think."

Tomorrow night, all of the most powerful supernaturals on this side of the globe would be gathered in the same castle. That was either a good thing for our enemies who could simply wipe us all out in one strike, or it could actually instill more fear in those who heard about how connected we all were.

We took the long path to exit the forest and strolled around the garden and the maze. It was still chilly here in the Northeast at this time of the year and I had heard someone commenting there might be a snowstorm coming.

"Now, tell me, how are you?" Farrah asked again.

I shrugged, and instead of answering the question directly, I told her about Levi. Not just what I had told Drake and the others about what had happened to me, and Elysium, and Ylena's betrayal. But how I had met Levi, how we had gotten tangled together, the magical bond, the first time we slept together, then finding out who his father was, leaving him behind after breaking the bond—or thinking we did.

Then meeting him again in the Great Eternity Hall, how now I thought it had been on purpose. Yes, he had been there to help with the loose creatures, but he would have left if it wasn't for me.

No? Was I reading too much into this.

But after the words he said to me, to Ylena, right before

sacrificing himself to stop her, I didn't know what to think anymore.

"He sounds like a big jerk," Farrah said. "One who obviously likes you."

"That's just the bond." That was my automatic response.

"You know Wyatt and I found out we were mates right before I set out to marry the enemy."

I nodded. "Oh, yeah. I remember that."

"At first, I told myself it was just the bond; we could ignore it. And even after, I pushed him away because of the curse." The curse the fae king had cast over all their kind—any fae who fell in love with another supernatural would lose their immortality. "I believed he deserved someone better."

"But you two are together and happy," I said.

"Yes, because we realized the bond isn't just fate. The bond knows the perfect pair for you, the one who completes you, even before you do. I believe that even without fate and the bond, actual fated mates would have found each other and fallen in love."

"But my bond was forced, it was an accident."

"You don't know that. Maybe fate had been working since before you and Levi were born, aligning your paths, so you would meet each other, and find a way to be together. Fate just gave it a push and helped you create an accidental bond with him."

I glanced at Farrah and narrowed my eyes. "Are you saying all of that to make me feel better?"

"No, really." She placed a hand over her heart. "I truly believe fated mates, or forced mates, whatever, would find and love each other without a bond."

I shook my head. "I'm not a romantic, Farrah. Don't try making me into one now."

"You might not be a romantic, but everyone likes a little romance in their lives. I know it."

I let out a sigh. "Regardless of the bond and how I might or might not feel about him, I want to find him. If he's trapped in the underworld, or dead, I need to find him. I owe it to him, to our bond."

"I know, and we'll find him."

"If only it was that easy."

I told her about the Great Eternity Hall, the girls who were there researching the underworld, and how I had started research here.

"I'll help you, Wyatt will help, and I'm sure we'll find other ways to do this." She bumped her shoulder on mine. "We always do."

"That is true." At least, I wanted to believe it was. Repeatedly, my friends and I had confronted big evils and dangerous situations, and even though it was never as smooth as we wished, we somehow made it.

We would make it again. We would find Levi, and we would save Elysium from a civil war that would disrupt everything and everyone.

"Now, let's get you to your room so you can shower." She plugged her nose. "You stink."

I bumped my shoulder on hers. "It isn't so bad, or you wouldn't have hugged me."

"Oh, I would. That's how much I have missed you." She gave me a soft smile. "But now I won't let you run away again." She pointed a finger at me. "I warn you. If you do, I'll hunt you down."

I smiled back at her, believing her, and loving her for being such a fierce, awesome friend.

5

To Farrah's delight, I not only took a shower, but I put on one of the fancy dresses in my closet. She loved dressing up, and, well, it made sense since everyone else in this castle was always ready for a ball.

We had dinner together in the main dining room—even the vampires, though they didn't need to eat. The table was full: Drake at the head with Thea to one side, Aurora to the other. Then the princes Dorian, Aston, Gray, princess Lyra and Prince Ward, Prince Killian, Lavinia, Wyatt, Farrah, Zadkiel, Elisa, Sally, and two other witches I had just met, Mila and Violet.

The food was delicious and I even allowed myself to drink a glass of wine, though I wanted to keep my mind sharp in case of trouble. We weren't foreseeing anything right now, but I had been too relaxed before when danger found us.

After dinner, we gathered in one of the largest sitting rooms. Lord Drake, the princes, the princess, and Prince Ward sat to one side, talking about some disturbance on the west coast, while the rest of us spread out on the other, talking about everything but our troubles.

Aurora entertained us all when she lifted her hands and neon butterflies sprouted from thin air and flew around us. We all stared at the little girl. She was a mystery to us all— sometimes she was just a kid, but sometimes she spoke as though she had the wisdom of an old witch. She had magic beyond anyone's comprehension, but she still had a lot to learn, especially when it came to control.

A neon blue butterfly landed on my shoulder, then it shuddered and disappeared.

The next morning, I woke up early and went to a training session with Zad before the day got busy. Farrah, determined to spend as much time as she could with me, tagged along. Unfortunately, this session wasn't any better than the last one, which only made me more frustrated.

"Tomorrow let's talk to the witches about your magic," Zad suggested as we made our way back to the castle for lunch.

After that, the castle was a flurry of movement as our friends and guests arrived for tonight's meeting.

Drake and Thea had arranged so maids were ready. Each group that arrived was escorted to their suites in the guests' wing, and then invited to join everyone in the larger sitting room on the castle's first floor.

Farrah stayed with me for a while, but Queen Kayden, her mate Fox, Farrah's brother, Daleigh, and Twyla arrived, and Farrah decided to be their host, dismissing the maids.

I had met Kayden and Daleigh years ago, right after meeting Farrah, and we had all become friends. Last year, I met Twyla. Lavinia and Killian had rescued us from the warlocks who wanted to take our powers. She was the daughter of the previous fae king, and because of that, people had hated her. So, we almost disappeared together. Two souls lost in the human world. But in the end, Farrah had gotten through to her and offered her a deal. Twyla proved she wasn't her father's daughter, helped them, and she was now a general in the Frost Court's army.

Daleigh, the lord of the Frost Court, was her fated mate.

I hadn't met Fox yet, though, Kayden's childhood friend, turned bodyguard, turned fated mate.

I frowned, realizing everyone had their own mates.

My bond had been forced, unnatural, not fate at all.

Or was it?

According to Farrah, everything was about fate. Meant to be.

"You're coming with us, right?" Farrah asked, bringing me back to the moment.

I gestured to myself. "I got out of training and I stink. I'll take a shower and find you later."

She gave me one suspicious look. Several times now I had promised to meet them later and ended up leaving without a goodbye.

"Don't worry, I won't run away." One corner of my lips tugged up. "Yet."

She fake-glared at me, but I knew she was still hurt about all of those times.

After promising again to see them later, I excused myself, went back to my room, took a shower, got dressed in a pretty gown, and instead of finding Farrah and her family and friends, I headed to the library. Knowing the evening was only going to get busier, I wanted a moment of peace and quiet and to do something for myself.

At the library, I tried getting my mind busy and researched more about the underworld.

So far, there weren't any real facts, everything was speculation. The only facts I had found were what we already knew: the underworld was another realm, larger than anyone knew, and the house of its king and his allies, which a few years ago was a supreme demon and his thousands, maybe millions, of demons.

Now, demon hunter Tanner was the king, and many of the demons had fled the underworld and were causing chaos in the human world.

As far as I knew, Tanner was assembling a team of warriors, and alongside the demon hunters, they were hunting these demons. To either kill or imprison them, it depended on their crimes and intentions.

Once upon a time, angels would be helping them.

But no. Ylena thought humans and all other supernaturals were plagues in this world. She wanted to eradicate them and start anew with a "purer" crop.

I put down my book and shook my head, still in shock. I had been under her wing for many years and I hadn't seen one hint, one clue. To me, she had been the most righteous, powerful, and right of all of us.

How wrong had I been.

"What's with the long face?"

I looked up and found Abbie, Maggie, and Lacey standing in front of me, and a maid behind them.

"Sorry, Ariella," the maid started. "They insisted on seeing you before I showed them to their rooms."

"We won't be using any rooms," Abbie said as she stepped forward and hugged me. "We'll portal out once the meeting is done."

I nodded to the maid, who spun on her heels and left.

"How are you?" Maggie asked me once she hugged me.

"Frustrated." I hugged Lacey next. "How about you? Have you found anything?"

"We've been researching almost nonstop since you left," Lacey said, "but when we think we find something, another book says something completely different."

"What do you mean?" I asked.

"Like, one book said the fiery pits aren't literal; it can mean the underworld in general, while another said the fiery pits is one single place where evil souls go to burn. And a third book said the fiery pits are several places, one more horrible than the other."

"There's no consensus on any information we've found so far," Abbie said.

"This sucks." I let out a long breath. "King Tanner is coming tonight. I haven't seen him in a while, but I'm sure he'll talk to me about this if I ask. As king, he might know the underworld better than anyone."

The girls nodded.

Tired of being stuck in this library, though it was a pretty impressive one, I took the girls on a quick tour through the castle.

Outside the library, we bumped into Erin and Rey, who the girls had already met. This time, Harvey, Ava, Claire, Harper, Doreen, and Andre, all demon hunters and close friends, accompanied them.

We stopped for a quick hi and introductions, but they continued toward their suites as the maid seemed eager to keep moving.

A few minutes later, while we were walking through winding corridors of the castle and admiring the beautiful artwork, we ran into Hazel, Sean, Evelyn, and Ash, and three others I didn't know.

The girls had met Evelyn and Ash, but not the others. I introduced the girls, and jokingly told them Hazel was the one who messed up the summoning spell and bound me to Levi. She was mortified, but Lacey reassured her it was for the best. That I had been a blessing to Levi.

Even if he was now in the underworld because of me.

Then Hazel told us about the other three: Brita, Anna, and Shade. Brita and Anna were witches and sisters, who had been alive for over five hundred years, and had been best friends with Hazel in her first life. Shade was Hazel's familiar, and he had been in her first life too.

Insane.

I asked them if they had heard from Kaz. I had given his number to Drake, and he said he tried calling, but Kaz wasn't answering.

"He's not coming," Evelyn said. She was a rare light witch with dark magic who could sense and use dragon magic. She had tried gaining the dragon shifters' trust, but that was a challenging thing to do. "I called him too, he didn't answer, but he texted back saying he was busy."

It was a shame the only dragon shifter we knew—those two old geezers that had been with Kaz last time I saw him didn't count—couldn't make the meeting. Kaz probably thought they were protected from any other evil in the world seeing as they lived on a hidden magical island. Hopefully, he was right.

We continued the tour for several more minutes and had made it to the maze, before bumping into Lord Drake, Queen Thea, and little Aurora.

"Lord Drake, Queen Thea, Princess Aurora, this is Abbigail, keeper of the Great Eternity Hall, her sister Magnolia, and Lacey, Levi's sister."

Drake shook Abigail's hand. "I've been at the Great Eternity Hall before. Long ago. The keeper's name was Alyssa."

Abbie nodded. "My great-grandmother."

I stared at the vampire. "You've been at the hall before?"

"A couple of times, actually," he said.

"Sounds like an interesting place," Thea said.

"Well, you're invited to come for a visit," Abbie told them.

"I would like that." Thea glanced at Aurora. "Wouldn't you?"

Aurora fixed her big green eyes on Abbie. "You're different."

Abbie frowned. "What do you mean?"

"Your magic," the girl said. "It's ancient, carried from generation to generation. And powerful." Aurora tugged at Thea's skirts. "Mommy, she's probably more powerful than you."

Thea smiled. "I bet she is."

"And you're pretty." Aurora looked at the other witches. "You all are."

"Aw, thank you," Maggie said. "You're pretty too."

"You can see magic," Abbie said. It wasn't a question.

"Sometimes, if it wants to be seen," Aurora said. "Sometimes, the magic hides. Like hers." She pointed to me. "I know your magic is inside you, but it's hiding from my view."

My brows curled down. "Why?"

Aurora shrugged. "Maybe it's shy?"

I looked at Abbie. "Maybe it's more ..."

Abbie nodded at me, probably thinking what I was thinking: We needed to investigate this.

"You're a bright witch," Abbie told Aurora.

"Thank you." The little girl smiled wide. "Mommy, can we go?"

"Of course, sweetie." Thea waved at us. "We'll see you later for dinner."

The two of them headed to the maze, but Lord Drake lagged behind.

"Aurora's words and magic are unique and we don't fully comprehend its extent yet," he said. "Most of the time, she can see and find things no one else knows. But sometimes, her magic fails."

"We should take heed of her words anyway and investigate," I said. Better safe than sorry.

He nodded. "I agree. You should. Just make sure you know this new clue can lead you down a road with no exit. I don't want you to be disappointed."

"I understand. Thanks for your concern."

He rested his hand on my shoulder before following his mate and their daughter into the maze. Apparently, they would spend some quality family time before the parents got stuck in a long meeting for hours.

As soon as Drake was gone, I turned to Abbie. "You can see magic too, right?"

"Not like that, no," Abbie said. "I can see things like fated mates' bond or other magical connections much clearer."

"But it seems the little witch was on to something," Lacey added. "We should probably look into it."

Maggie nodded. "I agree."

Shame it was already getting late, and the evening's event would start. Otherwise, I would take them back to the library right now.

What I did know was that this castle would be full of

powerful witches soon, and I could talk to a few of them about what Aurora had said.

After finishing the outside tour, I took the girls back inside the castle, where I showed them a few more places—the ballroom, the old throne room, which had been converted into a reception hall, Thea's workshop, and then my bedroom.

We spent another hour there, getting ready for the evening. I took another shower and changed into a beautiful black gown with a tight bodice. It wasn't as fancy as the gowns the others would be using, I was sure, but that was how I liked it.

Lacey pulled my silver-blond hair back and into an intricate braid, the long tail coming over my shoulder.

When I looked in the mirror after applying a little makeup, a pang cut through my chest. I actually looked pretty and Levi wasn't here to see it.

Since they hadn't come with any bags, Abbie opened a portal to the Great Eternity Hall. The girls stepped through and came out half an hour later in their gowns, makeup, and hairdo.

Supposedly, it was almost impossible to open portals inside the castle, but maybe Abbie and the hall were special and their magic different.

"Gwen, Britt, and Nate were mad at us for not bringing them," Maggie said.

I would probably have been too.

A few minutes prior to the appointed time, the girls and I started for the dining room where the events were located. On the way, we met with Farrah, Wyatt, Daleigh, Twyla, Kayden, and Fox. I introduced them to Abbie, Maggie, and Lacey.

Farrah hooked her arm through mine. "I heard you've taken good care of my best friend."

Abbie smiled at her. "She can be a little handful some-times, but we managed."

Everyone laughed and I pretended to glare at them.

"Thank you," Farrah said, heartfelt.

Together, we all walked to the dining room.

As expected, Drake and Thea were already there, along with Prince Dorian, Prince Aston, Prince Gray, Prince Killian, Lavinia, Princess Lyra, Prince Ward, Elisa, and Zadkiel.

I introduced the girls to the ones they hadn't yet met, while Farrah and her gang greeted the ones they hadn't yet seen.

Mila stood beside Lord Drake and Queen Thea and acted as a host, leading us to our places at the tables. And that was when I noticed the long rectangular tables were gone, replaced by large round tables that seated ten each.

She took the girls and me to a table right in the middle, and I wasn't surprised when I saw Farrah, Wyatt, Daleigh, Twyla, Kayden, and Fox arriving at the same table.

Though no one sat. A waiter arrived and offered us drinks. Each of us took a glass—I chose white wine—and we started small talk.

Kayden told me how she had gotten together with Fox—I had heard about it, but didn't know any details—and how it was to rule the kingdom after the tyrant Shadow King.

Also, they mentioned the rumors of a Shadow Prince hidden somewhere on Earth.

Twyla lifted her hands. "My father was as promiscuous as he was evil. He might have had several children."

"And you're concerned they will want the throne?" I asked.

"Technically, the throne belonged to the Blaze Court before the Shadow King took it by force," Fox said. "So even if they come, they have no official claim."

"But they sure will have allies," Kayden said. She explained a lot of Shadow fae were still upset they had lost their privileges since she took over.

"It's more than that," Daleigh added. "Because the Shadow King was evil, everyone is suspicious of them." He looked at Twyla, his mate. "Even Twyla has a hard time with it, and she has proven herself time and time again."

Twyla shrugged. "It doesn't bother me."

"It shouldn't," Kayden said. "Shadow fae are fae, just like the others. Hopefully, with time, this suspicion will go away."

"Hopefully, this Shadow prince won't decide he wants revenge and come back," Wyatt said. "That's the only way we'll have peace."

"I don't want to talk about this fake prince anymore," Kayden announced. She tipped her champagne glass and drank it to the last drop. "I know we're here on official business, but we're all together again, and that only happens once every blue moon. We should enjoy it and not talk about depressing topics."

"True," Fox added.

I grimaced, thinking of the topic Lord Drake and I would bring up later. That was not only depressing but worrying too.

They started talking about some festival they were planning for summer, and my attention shifted to the entrance, where Luana, Keeran, and Almae arrived.

I hadn't seen them yet, so I excused myself and met them as they finished greeting Drake and Thea.

Luana was the alpha of the Starlight Pack, a pack of wolf

shifters with amazing, magical powers. Her mate, Keeran, was the Warlock Lord, the most powerful warlock alive.

Almae was an old witch from the Silverblood coven, the same as Thea's, and she was Keeran's mother. She was powerful and had the gift of prophecies and visions, like Maggie, though the older witch had a lot more control and knowledge about it.

She was one of the candidates for me to talk to about my unstable magic. Though, not right now. I would seek her out after the meeting.

"How are you doing, dear?" Almae asked, sounding like a doting mother, as usual.

"I'm hanging in there," I answered honestly.

Luana also scolded me for disappearing, and Keeran joked about putting a GPS tracker on me.

Next, the demon hunters entered the room—Erin, Rey, Harvey, Ava, Claire, Harper, Doreen, and Andre. We had already seen them earlier, but after greeting the party hosts, the group approached us and we all formed a circle between the tables, the conversation flowing freely about several subjects at once.

Not long after, Hazel, Sean, Evelyn, Ash, Brita, Anna, and Shade arrived. I waved at them from my spot and they came to join us.

A few minutes later, the wolf shifters arrived. The Nightshade Alpha Shane, his mate. Raika, his brother and beta. Tyren, his other beta. Dom, and his mate. Anne, and Raika's sister, Ivy, and ... Thierry? The demon hunter?

After greeting Drake and Thea, Raika rushed to me and squeezed me in a tight hug. "Seriously, I had heard about your disappearing act, but I didn't think you would leave like that."

I pulled back, a little flustered for being put in the spotlight. "I had lost my magic. I was of no help to you guys. If I tried fighting, I would only end up messing it all up."

"Nonsense," Shane said. "You're a great fighter."

"Not against dozens of supernaturals when I'm powerless."

"But you have your magic back, right?" Tyren asked.

I nodded. "I do, but it's acting up. I'll tell you everything about it after dinner." Then I turned to Ivy and pointed to her hand in Thierry's. "What's going on there?"

Ivy smiled. "It's a long story."

"It's not that long," Thierry said.

She rolled her eyes. "Fine. We were on a mission, and we got stuck in a cabin in the mountains."

"Let me guess. Snowed in?"

"You got it," Thierry said.

"Well, the rest is history," Ivy said.

I smiled and shook my head. Only in our world would these surreal things happen.

Then I realized someone was missing. "Where's Minsi?" She was Shane's younger sister, who had crippling anxiety and some other problems. But even through all that, she was super sweet and kind.

"She's here actually," Shane said.

Raika nodded. "With Aurora." I had heard the two of them had a special friendship. "Rue and Sally are watching over them."

Oh, Rue was an old wolf shifter from their pack, kind and gracious, and like a grandmother to Shane, Raika, and their family.

"That's good," I said.

Last but not least, the two supernaturals I had been looking for arrived.

The king and the princess of the underworld were here.

6

—————

KING TANNER AND PRINCESS JASMIN WERE BOTH HALF DEMONS, and half siblings, and along with Erin, children of the previous king of the underworld, Brikan.

Tanner was a handsome twenty-something man, tall and broad, with brown curls and smooth, tanned skin, and Jasmin was stunning. She had luscious red hair, lots of feminine curves, and an exquisite face. She wore a tight black and burgundy gown that seemed to have been sewn to her body.

As a half-siren, she exuded sensuality and charm.

I tensed when they approached our group. As the rulers of the underworld, they probably could tell me about the fiery pits.

I waited until they greeted everyone to turn to them.

I opened my mouth to ask them about it, but Drake beat me to it.

"Friends, please take your seats," the lord of the castle said. "We'll have dinner before business."

Everyone spread out, taking their assigned places.

Maids brought out the first course, and the many vampires in the room got a big goblet filled with blood.

Once upon a time, that would have bothered me so much. But now I was used to it; I barely gave it a thought.

For some reason, as the courses were brought and empty plates were taken away, I started getting nervous. This meeting was supposed to be just to spread out information, to make sure no one fell for the angels' trap, something that almost happened to the demon hunters, and it was Thea's idea to use this meeting as an excuse to bring all of our friends and allies together.

But now that everyone was here, I felt tense.

Dessert was served—a delicious chocolate lava cake with caramel sauce—and as soon as most of the guests seemed done with it, Drake walked over to me.

He stopped behind my chair and whispered, "Ready?"

I nodded, though my nerves only increased.

I got up and walked with him to the center of the room, amid the five tables.

"Friends, we've called you all here tonight to see you all and have a good time," Drake started, "but also to clarify some rumors and explain some things. And give you some warnings." He gestured to me.

I cleared my throat. "Everyone here knows that five years ago I lost my wings and got stuck on Earth, since without wings, an angel can't cross the portal to go back to Elysium." I paused. "But that wasn't the only reason. I couldn't go back, because I knew the moment I stepped foot in Elysium, I would be captured and tortured ... until I gave them the information they wanted."

I saw many narrowed eyes, but I trudged on, and even

though a few people in here had already heard everything, I told them all about it.

I started with my mission, that I wasn't supposed to go—and now I knew why. The trap, the dagger, Molraz, my sword and my wings.

I briefly touched on meeting Farrah and Wyatt, Kayden and Daleigh, and so many others.

Then I slowed when I got to recent events: losing my powers to Paimon, being desperate about finding my wings and magic again. Summoning a wish-granting demon and trying to trick him to help me.

Getting my wings back, finding out my mentor, Ylena, had been behind it all, and no one had any idea. Slowly, she started gathering allies, who wanted to do the same things: to be stricter, to destroy all demons and most supernaturals, to make humans pay for being so careless and loving their free will.

I let them know that without a special item, Ylena couldn't kill Adona and take over. However, she was now stuck in the underworld with Levi, and I had no idea what Rhodes was doing in her absence.

Another thing I had no idea about was how Adona was doing. Was she trapped? Locked away? Did she know what was going on? How were the other angels? How long would it be until everything exploded and chaos ensued?

"I know they are smart and ready for anything," I said. "They tried scheduling a meeting with the demon hunters, and I'm pretty sure it was to either bring them to their side or kill them."

Murmurs started and I saw many of my friends shaking their heads, as if they couldn't believe this was happening.

Me neither.

"So, what do we now?" Erin asked. "I canceled the meeting, but they keep contacting us."

"By now, with their failed attempts to silence Ariella and with Ylena gone, Rhodes and their allies probably suspect Ariella told us everything," Drake said. "I doubt they will continue to bother you."

Erin nodded.

"We think Elysium is at the brink of a civil war," I said.

"One that will spill over to the human realm," Drake added.

"Right." I nodded. "And the first to be involuntarily involved in this war will be the demon hunters." They were viewed as the supernatural police, old allies of the angels, who once upon a time helped them with evil and darkness in the human realm. "Then it'll take over everyone and everything."

"So, we stop them," Shane suggested. "We go to Elysium, stop this Rhodes guy, and put an end to this rebellion."

"Only angels with their wings can enter Elysium," I reminded him.

"Right," he muttered. "Then we create a trap for him here?"

"That's on our list of possible outcomes," Drake said. "Friends, my intention with this meeting was to make you aware of what's going on, so you and your loved ones don't fall prey to the angels. We'll obviously do something, but we need more information and time to do so." He looked at me. "Ariella and I will create a council, with one or two of each supernatural species, and we'll assess the situation and come up with a plan about what to do. When we have a concrete plan, we'll invite everyone here again."

I frowned. Never would I have thought we would get to this point. Supernaturals rallying together to attack the angels.

What was wrong with this world?

Everyone nodded and muttered their agreements.

I looked at them all. "Thank you … for believing in me."

Farrah scoffed. "Was that even a question?"

I smiled. "Well, angels are trying to paint me as the villain. One against them all. I guess my worries are warranted."

"I see your point of view," Raika said, "but I agree with Farrah. We would never doubt you."

My heart swelled and the back of my eyes burned. I blinked rapidly, not wanting to cry in front of everyone.

"Now that this topic is out of the way," Drake said, "please, let's continue the festivities."

He gestured to a set of doors opening and musicians carrying string instruments entered the room. They settled in a corner and started playing. To my surprise, it was a popular, modern song and it sounded beautiful this way.

Drake squeezed my forearm, looked into my eyes, nodded at me once, and then turned to his table, where he offered a hand to Thea. With a smile, she took his hand and let him guide her to the other side of the tables, where there was more space for dancing.

Several emotions filled my chest at that moment. Gratitude for Drake and his unyielding presence. He had organized this whole shebang, and it seemed he would be on my side no matter what. Relief for my friends who never doubted me or my innocence.

And jealousy upon seeing Drake and Thea together.

And then of Shane and Raika, Hazel and Sean, Luana and Keeran, and all the other couples who headed to the improvised dance floor.

I went back to my table, grabbed my goblet of white wine, and drank half of it in one go.

To my dismay, the three single princes, Dorian, Aston, and Gray, came to our table, and took Abbie, Maggie, and Lacey to dance.

I was alone.

But only for a moment.

I glanced at the table to the side and found Tanner and Jasmin still seated, talking among themselves in hushed tones.

With my glass in hand, I walked up to them. "May I sit?"

"Of course." Tanner pulled out the chair beside his.

"How are you two doing?" I asked as I sat, trying to be polite.

"I would be better if this party had a lot of hot men I could cling to," Jasmin said. She glanced at her brother. "Right?"

Tanner rolled his eyes. "She fed before coming here, but it's still the only thing she talks about."

"Well, we're in a room full of beautiful, powerful supernaturals," she said. "Can you blame me for being turned on? And when I'm turned on, I burn through the energy faster."

As a siren, Jasmin needed to consume a male's soul every few days to survive. I knew that Thea, Almae, and other witches had tried spells to keep her from killing her victims or even needing their energy.

But it had only backfired and made her sick for weeks.

"Ignore her," Tanner said. "Good call on the meeting-slash-dinner. It has been a while since I have seen some of our friends." He gestured to Lacey, Abbie, and Maggie. "And some I didn't know."

I had introduced the girls to them before but hadn't gone into detail about it. "They've helped me out a lot in the past few weeks."

"You've been through a lot," Jasmin said. Though her words conveyed sympathy, her tone was indifferent.

"Yes, and I might need your help," I said. Tanner raised his eyebrows. "You heard that Levi took Ylena to the underworld. I think he's trapped there and I would like to get him out. And I thought—"

Jasmin picked up her glass of champagne. "You thought we can just pluck him out of there."

"Well, it's probably not as simple as that, but as the rulers, you two probably know that place better than anyone and—" The two of them started laughing. I just stared, appalled. "Did ... did I say something funny?"

"Not funny." Jasmin took a deep breath to calm down and stop laughing. "Just painfully true."

I was confused. "What?"

Tanner let out a deep sigh. "We took over four years ago, and we've barely explored ten percent of the underworld."

"That's what we were told," Jasmin said. "If the underworld is bigger than our informant says, then it could be as little as five percent."

"Or one percent," Tanner said. "I don't trust our informant that much."

I opened my mouth, but nothing came out.

"Disappointing, right?" Jasmin found another glass of champagne and took a sip. "Believe me when I say, no one is as disappointed as we are."

"I don't say this to anyone, but it has been a ... difficult reign," Tanner admitted. "We are young and still newbies in a place we don't know, filled with our enemies, who are hiding and waiting to strike."

I didn't know why I thought they would know the place, or at least maybe most of it. Shouldn't the rulers know everything about their world? I had assumed ...

"So, you have no idea what the fiery pits are? Where it could be?" I knew the answer, but I couldn't stop the questions from coming.

"Sorry, Ariella, but we don't," Tanner said.

"But now that we know about your man and his evil mother, we'll keep an eye out for him," Jasmin said.

That didn't sound like enough, but there wasn't much I could do.

"Thanks," I muttered. Slowly, I got up and my brain registered Jasmin's words.

Your man.

I opened my mouth to tell her he was not my man, but then Tanner offered his hand to her. "Care to dance, dear sister?"

She looked at his hand, almost disgusted, but sighed. "Since there's nothing better to do."

I watched as the two of them joined the others for a dance.

Tyren had taken Almae to the dance floor, while Shade took Doreen.

I was the only one left.

My heart squeezed, thinking of Levi, and also of the other times I felt I didn't fit in. I was the spare tire of our entire community.

I took a deep breath and reminded myself that wasn't the

case. I did fit in and my friends would help me, and somehow everything would be all right.

But right now, I didn't feel like staying here.

I left the room and went to bed.

7

—————

"Sweetheart, wish for me to take her to the fiery pits of the underworld."

Levi jumped, grabbed Ylena, and disappeared into a portal.

And before the portal closed, I jumped in …

Into darkness.

My heart racing, I gave it a couple of seconds, but my eyes didn't adjust. Everything was pitch black.

"Levi?" I called.

Nothing. No sound. No sight. No smell.

I took a few careful steps, my hands outstretched in front of me.

Then suddenly, a scream filled the air around me.

A cliff appeared three feet from me and raging fire billowed up, up, up … to the infinite dark sky. The heat licked at my skin, and I recoiled.

The scream echoed again and this time I saw the shape inside the fire. A large figure, with curling horns atop his head, and wide bat-like wings.

A demon.

Levi.

I started forward, but the fire exploded up again, pushing me back.

The fire didn't let up, but Levi became more visible and I could see the flames burning his skin, his wings, his entire self. He thrashed and screamed, a guttural, deep sound that hurt my soul.

"Levi," I muttered, desperate.

How could I save him? What could I do?

His black eyes met mine and he stretched his hand toward me. He was several yards away, but I needed to get to him. I stretched my arm.

The flames erupted again, catching my bare arm.

I screamed.

I sat up in bed with a jerk, breathing hard, my skin slick with sweat.

Holy shit, it had been a dream.

A nightmare.

By the light, I hoped that wasn't true. That what I had seen had been only my imagination, manifesting all of my fears, and nothing else.

I glanced at my phone on the nightstand. Shit, it was just past five in the morning. Way too early to start the day. But I knew that I wouldn't be able to go back to sleep now.

I got up, took a quick shower to wash the sweat off my body, brushed my teeth, put on practical training clothes, and went to the kitchen to find some breakfast.

At this time, the castle was almost silent, pitched in darkness, with only the occasional vampire guard making their rounds, and the ones posted at entrances.

The kitchen wasn't as silent, though. A couple of humans, and two low-ranked vampires, were already getting started on breakfast—with the castle full of guests, they needed to start early.

The scent of cinnamon and vanilla hung heavy in the air.

"How can I help you, *ma chérie*?" Chef Morris asked.

"Just let me raid whatever you're making, and I'll be out of here," I told him.

"If you wait five minutes, I'll make you a real breakfast."

I wanted to tell him that wasn't necessary, but I had learned long ago he wouldn't let this go. So, I agreed and he gave me a plate with heaps of pancakes, scrambled eggs, bacon, and a big mug of coffee.

It was enough to feed five of me. "Thank you, Morris. You're the best."

The old man waved me off, and I got the hint. He wanted me out of his kitchen. Happy to oblige, I carried my food out. I would go to the training grounds, sit in a corner, and eat before starting with light exercises.

However, as I walked down the hallway, heading to the foyer, I heard a soft voice singing. It came from one of the sitting rooms, where the light was dim and the door was halfway open.

Curious about who would be singing at this time, I spied inside.

Thea lifted her head, her voice faltering for a second, but she waved at me and continued. Carefully, I entered the room and saw Aurora curled on the sofa beside Thea, her head on her mother's legs. Thea ran a hand up and down the girl's back as she breathed in deeply.

"Hi," I said softly.

"Couldn't sleep?" Thea asked me in a whisper.

I put the plate and the mug down on the center table and took a seat on the armchair to her right.

"I could ... until I couldn't." I took a piece of bacon and gestured for her to take one too. "Please, Morris gave me more than I can eat."

She smiled. "He always does." Thea reached to the plate and got a strip of bacon. "Thanks."

"What about you two? Couldn't sleep either?"

"Didn't you feel it? Aurora had another night terror. The entire castle shook. It wasn't the worst she's had, but I bet most people woke up with it."

It was probably during my nightmare. I shook my head. "No, I didn't."

I looked at the little girl, now sleeping peacefully. She looked like a porcelain doll. Unfortunately, she'd started having night terrors where her power escaped her, and she caused the entire castle to shake. Drake and Thea had been really worried about them, afraid that at some point, she would cause the castle to collapse.

Since then, Thea had warded Aurora's room to keep her power contained, but that didn't stop the night terrors from causing an earthquake.

"After she calmed down, she couldn't go back to sleep, so I came down here with her," Thea told me.

"And she fell asleep."

"Of course she did." She glanced at her daughter, adoration stamped on her pretty face. "All I have to do is make her comfortable, sing, and done. She crashes again."

"You guys will figure this out," I said.

Thea looked at me. "I hope so, but so far, no one has, and our friends are the most powerful supernaturals we know."

"And she's the most powerful of all."

Thea nodded. "That scares me."

"I know." I thought of getting up and giving her a big

squeeze, but I wasn't the emotional type and I would probably wake Aurora if I tried. "She'll do well, though, whatever her destiny is."

Thea looked away and wiped under her eyes. I would never know the love a mother had for their children, seeing as I couldn't have my own, but I knew it was supposed to be something so vast and so intense, it was inexplicable. It was one's heart out of their chest.

And for a brief moment, I envied them.

But I had no time to cry about something I couldn't change.

Thea and I ate half of the food on my plate. When we were done, I stood, holding the plate to take it back to the kitchen, but she told me to leave it there and someone would pick it up later.

I put the plate down. "I'm off to train."

She glanced out the window. The sun was finally rising and bathing the landscape in golden light. "I'm not sure what time Zad will be up, but I'll let him know where you are."

"Thanks."

With a wave of my hand, I walked away and went to the training grounds.

Outside, a frigid wind greeted me, and I lifted my head to the sunlight coming from the horizon. I stopped halfway and took a deep breath. Here, I could pretend everything was well, and that everything would work out.

Because it had to.

Inside the training center, I started with easy stretches and yoga-based moves, since I had just had breakfast. But after that, I warmed up by running around the track. My intention was to run for thirty minutes, rest for another thirty, and then start with my magic, even if it was something simple like playing with a small bolt between my hands.

But ten minutes into my run, Zad entered the place.

He stood beside the track and I slowed down until I was right in front of him.

"I thought you would be here," he said.

"Isn't it too early for you?" I asked.

He shook his head. "No, I knew you would be eager to continue."

"I am."

He pulled his blond hair into a tight ponytail. "Let's train."

THE NEXT WEEK WAS HELL.

I trained with Zad almost every morning and afternoon, for several hours at a time, and I hadn't improved one bit. Well, that wasn't true. I could access my magic a little faster, control it for a little longer, and aim better.

But my magic still fought against me and that made me exhausted.

And frustrated.

The day after the meeting, most supernaturals traveled home. Although, Farrah and Wyatt stayed.

"I'm not letting you out of my sight anymore," Farrah warned me.

"She's serious," Wyatt said, sounding mildly annoyed.

I could relate. Farrah was treating me like a teenager who couldn't make the right decisions.

I confess, there were moments when that was nice, but most of the time the attention was too much.

Almae, Keeran, and Luana also stayed for another day, along with Lacey, Abbie, and Maggie.

After what Aurora said about my magic, we wanted to do a checkup on me, and we needed powerful witches and warlocks.

The afternoon after the meeting, Thea gathered us in her workshop, including Lavinia, who despite being more than a witch, was powerful too.

They drew a witch's circle and put me in the middle.

I didn't have the best experience with those, but I obliged them.

Then they cast spells and tried to see the magic within me.

"I can see it, but I can't really see it," Lavinia said.

"Yes," Almae agreed. "I can sense the magic, I know it's there, but like Aurora said, it's hiding."

"It must have been traumatic for your magic to have been ripped from you," Keeran said. He closed his eyes and took a deep breath. "And I'm sure it was traumatic for you too."

Understatement of the year.

"That could be something," Thea said. "The magic is protecting itself."

"But isn't my magic part of me?" I asked, confused. "It shouldn't be protecting itself from me. It should embrace me and protect us, together."

At some point, Thea brought in Aurora. Though she tried leaving her daughter out of supernatural business, Thea knew there was no one like Aurora.

The little girl looked straight to my gut. "It's dark. There's light, but it's dark. That's all I see."

I nodded, trying not to get irritated with a nine-year-old.

It wasn't her fault. She was too young, with too much power she didn't yet know how to control.

Thea promised to talk to her later, see if some lesson about blocked or hidden magic sparked any ideas, and help Aurora understand what she was seeing so she could actually tell us.

After being a guinea pig for them more than two hours, the witches gave up.

For now.

"We'll research," Almae assured me. "We'll bring your magic to its full glory again."

Well, they might not be able to do it, but I knew they would try their hardest, and that alone made me proud to be their friend.

It would suck if they failed, though.

The next day, Zad and I resumed training, because according to him, "Maybe all your magic needs is to familiarize with you and what you can do. Remind it. And for that, you need to keep using it."

So, we kept training.

I only grew frustrated.

I felt like nothing was happening, nothing changed.

Drake had a web of spies and allies, and he told me he was trying to infiltrate Elysium, if not physically, then through connections and info, but everyone was quiet and unapproachable. It was as if they were on high alert now that Ylena was gone.

Once more, I wondered if the snake had lost its head and was now thrashing aimlessly, or if Rhodes had taken the helm and was trudging along with their plan.

Which involved securing the dagger.

I was on my way to another afternoon training session with Zad when a young page approached me.

"Lord Drake would like a word," he said.

"Right now?"

"If possible."

Of course it was. He was sort of the leader of our whole community, the king. We didn't deny his requests, even when they weren't forced.

"Can you tell Zad I'll be late for training, please?"

"Of course." He bowed to me as if I was some kind of noble lady and dashed away down the hallway.

I changed directions. I paused in front of the study's doors and knocked.

"Enter," Drake said from the inside.

I opened the door and found him standing behind his desk, watching something through the big window. Today, he was wearing a light gray shirt, buttoned up to his elbows, and black slacks, but the black jacket and burgundy tie were draped behind his chair, which told me, he had started the day in a suit.

Always looking ready for a ball.

Blue sparks jumped up outside the window and the corner of Drake's mouth tugged up.

A second later, a faint, but happy shriek followed by laughter came from the garden below the window.

"Aurora?" I asked.

He nodded and turned to me, the half-smile still on his lips. "She saw a butterfly, so she created hundreds of others and sent them flying around the garden."

"I know you hear this a lot, but she's already so powerful."

He nodded again and sat down on his chair. "She is and that scares me. It scares Thea too."

"I know. I wish I could offer you some words of wisdom, but I've got nothing. All I can say is that whatever happens in her future, you know we'll all be here for her."

"I appreciate that." He leaned back in his chair and pinned his gaze to me, his whole stance changing from relaxed to businesslike. "Ariella, I'll get directly to the point. This Scarlet Hex Dagger seems to be powerful and I want to make sure it's well hidden."

I knew this would come up at some point. I was surprised Drake hadn't talked to me about the dagger earlier.

"I can't say it's super well hidden," I confessed. "I was alone, running for my life, afraid of my own shadow ... I didn't have many choices. I hid it and left. I never went back, afraid it would lead others to it." I sure hoped it was still there.

"I understand, but you're not alone now. If it's not well hidden, don't you think it's time to go back, take it, and hide it in a safe place this time? We have a secure vault underneath the castle, and there's also the Grand Eternity Hall."

I pressed my lips tight. Long ago, Thea broke into that secure vault, and the dagger had been stored at the hall before being taken by Molraz. But I knew that had been extraordinary situations, and that they would now take more precautions, cast more wards, and make the place more secure.

The Scarlet Hex dagger had once belonged in the Great Eternity Hall; maybe it was time it returned to its rightful place.

I nodded. "All right. I'll—"

My phone vibrated in my pocket. I usually left it silent, but it still vibrated. Frowning, I picked it up and stared at the screen.

"I don't know this number," I said, turning the phone to Drake.

"But I do. You'll want to take that."

I pressed the green button on the screen and said, "Hello?"

"Ariella, hi, this is Tanner," the king of the Underworld said.

I sat straighter, suddenly tense. "Tanner, hi. What happened?"

"I might have a lead for you."

8

———

TANNER DIDN'T TELL ME ANYTHING ON THE PHONE, ONLY THAT I would want to come to the underworld at my earliest convenience. It would have been right that instant, but Drake put a leash on me.

"Whatever Tanner has for you, you don't know what to expect," he said. "I'll put a team together to go with you."

I started to protest, but when he looked at me with those intense eyes, like two green flames full of power and strength, I was reminded why he was the unnamed leader of us all.

"But what about the dagger?" I asked, knowing that was important too.

"Levi is your mate," he said. "We rescue him first, then worry about the dagger."

Though I knew he was talking from experience—he would do anything for Thea—my chest expanded with gratitude.

Drake told me to meet the team in the foyer in two hours. I left his office and went to the training grounds where Zad was waiting for me.

I told him what had happened.

"I'll talk to Drake," he said. "I'm coming with you."

I was on my way back to my room to pack—I had no idea if we were going there for an hour or a week—when I almost bumped into Farrah and Wyatt in the hallway.

"There you are!" Farrah smiled at me. "I was going to the training grounds now. Did you guys finish early today?"

I shook my head and told them about the new plans; they wanted in. Apparently, we would arrive in the underworld with an army.

I hoped Tanner's lead was a good one.

After taking a quick shower and changing into a clean uniform—I wanted to be prepared in case of a fight—I packed a small backpack with extra clothes and marched downstairs to the foyer.

Drake, Thea, Aurora, all the princes and princess and their respective partners, Elisa and Zadkiel, Farrah and Wyatt, and Keeran and Luana were here. There were also a handful of lower-ranked vampires who I didn't know well.

"Everyone is coming with me?" I asked as I approached them.

"No," Drake said. "Zadkiel, Farrah, Wyatt, Frank, and Cyran, and I are coming."

My brows slammed down. "Shouldn't you stay here? The castle needs you." And everyone else in the supernatural world.

"It's okay," he said. "Thea will stay and she can take over for a few days."

"I already do half of the work," she said with a wink.

"More than half," Prince Aston said with a cough.

"Well, that's probably true," Drake agreed. Drake had fixed his shirt and put on his jacket and tie. The lord of the castle gestured to a page, who opened the front doors. "We're waiting on one more."

As if on cue, a portal opened outside the doors, and Lacey stepped through it. "Am I late?"

"You're just in time," Drake told her.

The portal closed and she walked up to me. "Surprise!"

"What the hell are you doing here?" I asked, as a protective feeling came over me. I didn't want her to come with us, because I knew it would be dangerous.

"You're going after my brother and I'm coming with you," she said simply. I glanced back at where the portal had been a second ago. "Abbie can't come because she needs to stay with the hall. Maggie wanted to, but Abbie forbade her."

"Good," I muttered. "One less person for me to worry about."

Drake cleared his throat. "Everyone ready?"

I nodded, and some answered out loud.

Then Keeran stepped forward and I understood why he had come: to open a portal for us to the nearest underworld entrance.

Zadkiel said goodbye to Elisa, while Drake hugged Thea and Aurora. Farrah and Wyatt crossed the portal, then Frank and Cyran.

Lacey and I started for the portal, but Aurora reached for my hand. I stopped and looked at her. "Everything okay, pretty girl?"

"The darkness is there," she said, sounding older than she was. "It's always there, but it'll spread and come with. Be aware of the darkness."

"Aurora?" I asked.

"What was that, sweetie?" Thea asked.

"I don't know," she said, her voice back to her childish one. "I could only see black everywhere."

Over Aurora's head, Thea met my gaze. "I'll try to find out what it means and I'll let you know."

I nodded, and after squeezing Aurora's hand, I crossed the portal. Lacey stepped through next.

Drake was the last one. He signaled to Keeran, who dropped his chin once, then closed the portal.

Keeran had sent us to a place I had been before—the gate outside Winnipeg. Right now, we were in an empty field that went on for miles with a large stone the size of a three-story building dead center. But I knew that if I walked several feet in any direction, an illusion would appear and I would find myself in the middle of a farm, complete with a farmhouse, a barn, and extensive fields ready for planting.

A dozen Blackthorn Hunters guarded the large stone wall, and two of them stood directly at its side. As we approached, they touched the wall at the same time and a green line appeared from their hands. It swirled over the stone until it met in the center and grew, becoming one large, green mesh shining bright.

We crossed the portal and the world shimmered for a second, then settled once more.

A black path opened in front of us, flanked by hot red lava, its heat palpable. Above us, the sky was dark gray, and beyond the path was a huge black palace with several endless turrets sprawled over the dark landscape. Lightning cut across the sky, casting larger-than-life shadows everywhere.

I had heard King Tanner and Jasmin had done everything to tone down the menace and creepiness of this place, but its magic was so ancient and strong, nothing worked.

"This way," Drake said, taking the lead across the path cutting through the lava.

As we approached the castle, I saw a handful of demon hunters standing by the giant double doors. They nodded at Drake and turned their attention back to the horizon. I frowned, confused for a minute, wondering why they didn't open the doors for us.

But then they opened by themselves.

Inside, the foyer was as large as a ballroom and as dark as the outside. Black stone, dark gray walls, dark crystal chandeliers, dark framed mirrors on the walls.

We crossed under an archway into a wide hallway. At the end, another set of double black doors greeted us. Once more, the doors opened by themselves, and behind them a female smiled at us.

"Welcome to the underworld," she said. I was certain she was a demon; I just didn't know what kind. "I'm Lily, King Tanner's assistant." She gestured for us to come in. "Please, come with me."

We followed Lily through the door into a large room. At the end of the room were two thrones made of black marble, one slightly smaller than the other. King Tanner sat on the largest one, while Jasmin was on the other.

When they saw us approaching, they stood.

"Thank you, Lily," Tanner said. Then, he glanced at our group and smiled. "Welcome to the underworld."

"Are we having a party?" Jasmin asked, her eyes alight. "I would have prepared the ballroom."

"The underworld has a ballroom?" Lacey asked.

Jasmin nodded. "It has everything."

"King Tanner," Drake started, his deep, serious voice echoing through the large room and bringing everyone to attention. "It was my idea to bring a large party to the underworld. If your lead turns out to be a good one, I didn't want to waste time putting a team together."

"I understand." Tanner reached forward and swept his hand from left to right. Chairs made of shadows appeared behind us, forming an arc in front of the thrones. "Please sit. I don't like to talk with my friends as if they were my subjects."

We all took a seat, but I couldn't settle. "What did you find?"

Tanner glanced to his left as a man entered the room from a side doorway. He was tall and broad, with cropped blond hair and a mean face. He wore black leather that looked like a modified demon hunter's uniform, and he sported a bow across his back.

"This is Rage," Tanner said. "He's a half demon, half demon hunter like me. A couple of months ago, he joined us to explore the underworld." He stared at Zad. "Unlike a certain angel."

Zad took it in stride. "When you asked, I had other priorities."

"Did you complete those priorities?" Jasmin asked and Zad nodded. He wanted revenge against the angel who had imprisoned him in the underworld for twenty years. "Are you ready to join us now?"

Zad shook his head. "I apologize, but I think my place is with Lord Drake and DuMoir Castle."

"Can't blame you," Tanner said. "Things here are complicated."

"What does any of that have to do with your lead?" I asked, my patience running thin.

Tanner looked at me. "I'm getting there." He moved his hand again and this time a table that was at least twelve feet long and eight feet wide appeared before us, and on top of the table was a dark, magical map of a place I had never seen before.

The underworld.

Curious, I stood and approached the table to get a better look. Everyone loomed over the table as well. The map was a wonder in itself. It seemed made of moving shadows, and if I stretched up and crouched down, I could see the elevations.

Unfortunately, only the center was well defined, with this castle built of shadows in great detail. The immediate area around it was on the map, and then just another two sections were drawn and named, both of them a little bigger than the center and directly south of the castle.

The rest was plain dark clouds, though some had hard lines separating them.

"When we took over—" Tanner said, his voice closer. I looked up and saw him, Jasmin, and Rage on the other side of the table. "—the underworld was a mess."

"It still is," Jasmin muttered.

"The demons residing here ran rampant, either to other corners of the underworld, or to Earth," Tanner went on. "Some even tried taking the castle, but thankfully, the demon hunters had come with us and made sure we had the castle and the entire area cleared."

"Apart from Lily and Moth," Jasmin said.

"Right. Lily and Moth are two lower demons. They've proven themselves loyal to us."

"Lily served as a maid, so she knew most of the castle's secret passages and what was where," Jasmin said. "While Moth was a servant for Brikan. He was the fly on the wall on several of his meetings, though he admits that he was afraid and never really paid attention to what was going."

"However, he seems to remember some details about the land," Tanner said. He pointed to the map. "He told us that the castle is the center, and that the entire underworld is twice the size of Earth."

"With a lot less water and more land." Jasmin shuddered. "Dry, brittle, dead land."

"Anyway, Rage here is looking over the exploration of the underworld with a few trusted demons," Tanner continued. "He started exploring this section." The king gestured to a large area on the upper part of the map. "Tell us about it, Rage."

Rage nodded once. "Right now, we believe this area is probably the size of Asia. But it could be bigger." His voice was deep, which definitely gave out warrior vibes. "A couple of days ago, I encountered demons here." He pointed to where the section met another. "They were hiding, but harmless, afraid of all the changes and what it meant for them. They told me they saw a big ball of fire with some weird, moving shapes fall from the sky in this direction." He pointed to the middle of the section. "An explosion followed, and then everything went quiet. Usually, I go inch by inch, registering everything so we can map it out, but King Tanner told me about your predicament." He glanced at me. "So, I went directly to that area."

I held my breath. "And?"

"It opens to a big cliff with mist at the bottom," Rage said. "But I saw a trail of scorched earth where the ball of fire could have touched before falling into the mist."

"And you're assuming this ball of fire was Levi and Ylena?"

"It's a stretch, but it matches the timing. Plus, this cliff and whatever is down there seems like a prison for dangerous demons."

"Something like fiery pits," I muttered.

Rage nodded. "Exactly."

"When Rage told us about it, I knew I had to tell you," Tanner said.

I looked at him. "Thank you."

"In all honesty," Tanner continued, "if I didn't know you were looking for your demon, I would have probably told Rage to continue exploring everything around the cliff and leave that for last. But knowing you're after your demon, I offer you a chance to go down into the mist and search for him."

My demon.

I wish.

I looked at my friends. They all stared straight at me, unmoving, unbreakable, as if nothing I said would change their minds.

"Remember," Rage said. "This seems to be a prison, and we have no idea what we'll meet at the bottom."

"You're coming with us?" I asked, a little surprised. I don't know why I wasn't expecting that.

He stood even taller, his chest puffed. "Sure am. I'm the first of King Tanner's warriors and the current explorer. It's my duty to go into the mist and map it out."

"I'm okay with that," I said.

"I'll go too," Tanner said.

"What? No!" Jasmin almost shrieked. "We've had this conversation. You're the new king of this place. Many of those demons want to kill you. Do you want to make it easy for them?"

"They want to kill the previous king of the—"

"Do you think that matters to them?"

"Perhaps it doesn't, but—"

"You're not going!"

"Don't tell me what to do!"

"I'm your sister and second in command and—"

"I agree with the princess, King Tanner," Rage said, interrupting the two. I had heard about their bickering, but this was the first time I had witnessed it. I had to admit it was quite entertaining.

"Me too," Drake said.

Tanner almost glared at him. "You're like a king to your coven and you're going down there!"

"I've been the lord of DuMoir Castle for a while now," Drake said, "and I've trained Thea and the princes to take over and remain in power, in case I'm gone. Your rule, though, is still new and unstable. You need to make sure it only grows stronger, and you can't do that if you put yourself at risk."

Tanner's glare intensified. "Fine. I won't go. But when you're back, Lord Drake, we need to discuss an idea I have for these rampant demons."

Drake nodded. "So we shall."

"He's not going, but I am," Jasmin announced.

"What?" Tanner almost shouted.

She glared at him. "Do not start arguing with me again."

Tanner huffed but kept his mouth shut.

I let out a sharp breath. "Is that settled? Can we go now?"

Rage looked at Tanner. When his king nodded, the warrior nodded too. "If you're ready, we can leave now."

9

 INSISTED WE STOP BY THE CASTLE'S DINING room and have an early lunch, even if for ten minutes.

"You don't know how long you'll be down there, or what you'll find," Tanner said.

I wanted to go now, but I could see his reasoning. So instead of complaining, I followed everyone to the dining room, where the food was already being served—juicy steak cut in thin slices, baked potatoes with herbs, and several other roasted vegetables.

"I apologize for it being so simple," Jasmin said at the head of the long table. Tanner sat at the other one. "But we weren't expecting so many of you."

This might be simple to them, but it was delicious.

Besides, not everyone ate the food. Drake and his vampires had goblets full of blood instead.

In my eagerness to get moving, I was the first done. Thankfully, no one was here to have fun, so they all finished right after me. Except for Tanner. He ordered the servants to bring more wine and serve dessert. He bid us good luck as we exited the room.

Jasmin went out through another door, but a few seconds later, as we filed out of the castle, she reemerged in a demon hunter's uniform.

Seriously, if one day I settled somewhere, I needed a magical closet that always knew the guests' sizes and did quick changes like that.

Outside the castle, Rage reminded us that even though Princess Jasmin was with us, he was the head of this mission and whatever he said, went. If something attacked us and he told us to run instead of fighting, we didn't question him. We just ran.

Sure, whatever.

We exited the castle through the back where a black brick bridge stretched above the lava. The heat was even worse than when we arrived, and it would have bothered me, if I wasn't a pile of nerves.

By the light, we had a lead. A real lead to Levi. We would find him, I was sure of that.

Farrah noticed how tense I was and hooked her arm through mine, offering me a small smile as we crossed the bridge. She didn't have to say anything, and honestly, I didn't want her to. Her presence here, her support, was enough.

The bridge took us to an open area of dry, gray earth. There were dark mountains to the right, and thick clouds and lightning to the left. This place didn't seem like a prize, but something to be conquered, ruled, and controlled. It looked like a prison through and through. The stuff of nightmares.

I didn't envy Rage for exploring it, and Tanner and Jasmin for ruling it.

"The trek is long," Rage warned us. "But we have rides."

To the side, ten horses made of shadows materialized. They were huge, certainly a foot or two bigger than any other horse on Earth. Thicker too, with strong legs and square muzzles. Their eyes were red and their long, luscious black mane and tail moved as if there was a fan in front of them.

The horses approached us, the clop of their hooves echoing on the dry terrain. Rage reached for the first one, Princess Jasmin got the second, and Lord Drake had the third. The rest of us spread around the horses. I walked up to one of the beasts, admiring its beauty and also a little concerned on how easily it could squash me if it wanted to.

The horse lowered his front legs, and as I held on to his mane and swung my leg, a small black saddle appeared on its back. Once I was seated, the horse straightened and stood there.

I was about to kick it on the sides to see if I could get it to move, but then Rage brought his horse around and addressed the party.

"The area we're going is far," he said. "The horses will move fast, faster than horses in the human realm, faster than a car, so hold on tight."

With that, he and his horse took off.

The other horses followed. At the first movement, I almost fell off my horse, but I held on to the reins and kept my legs pressed against its side. I hadn't ridden in a while, and not this kind of magical horse, but after a minute or so, it got easier.

What was the human phrase? Just like riding a bike. If the bike was enchanted and went a lot faster than others.

Rage and Drake took the lead, and somehow, the two were able to talk, in spite of the speed. Princess Jasmin was right behind them, followed closely by Zad, Frank, and

Cyran. Wyatt was next, and then it was Farrah, Lacey, and me at the back.

At first, Farrah tried talking to us too, but it was impossible. The horses moved too fast and sometimes they jerked to the side to avoid an obstacle or jump over a stream or some fallen branches. We had to be prepared for everything.

We rode in almost complete silence for about three hours. It was close to four when Rage lifted his fist and the horses all stopped on their own. We formed a messy circle so we could all hear him.

"It's almost five in the afternoon, your time," Rage said. "We can rest now, or we can keep moving and stop later."

I glanced up to the dark sky. It was pitch black, with no stars. I wondered how this entire place wasn't completely dark. Instead, it looked like a cloudy evening, where everything was dark gray.

"How long until we reach the cliff?" Jasmin asked, squirming over her horse.

"Another four hours or so," Rage said.

"I suggest we reach the cliff," Drake said with his "lord" voice, which left room for little discussion. "We rest there for a couple of hours before going down."

I was fine with that, especially because when we arrived at the cliff, I would push for us to keep moving. I knew that I wouldn't be able to rest until we found Levi, much less sleep.

We all agreed to it and kept moving.

Four hours later, we arrived at the cliff. The horses didn't get too close to it, though. We dismounted them and they instantly faded away.

"What the—" Wyatt said, looking around.

"They won't go with us down the cliff?" Lacey asked.

Rage shook his head. "They don't want to. Which tells you how terrible things probably are down there."

I walked up to the edge of the cliff and looked down. It was dark here, but way, way down, there was smoke, a cloud of thick mist, and nothing. The cliff extended endlessly to my right and my left, and beyond, there was the mist. It touched the horizon and blended in with the dark sky.

"This is Barnoch and Millmor," Rage said, catching my attention. I turned and saw as two men approached the party.

"Or Barn and Mill for short," Jasmin said, sounding bored.

"They are lesser demons who signed up to help us explore the underworld," Rage continued. "They are on my team and will help us in the mist."

They both said hello and Rage told them all of our names.

"All right," Drake said. "We should rest now."

I shifted my weight. "I know it's late, but I'm fine. Aren't you all fine? Don't you want to keep going and get this over with soon?"

I was hoping to find support in Lacey and Farrah, but Lacey yawned, and Farrah looked at me as if she was debating buying this fight or not.

"Ariella ..." It was Drake who spoke. "I know you're eager to go, but we should rest and regain our energy. We don't know what we'll find down there."

"But—" I pressed my lips tight.

"Remember, if this is Levi, then he has already been down here for a few days," he said, his voice gentler than usual. "He can wait a few more hours."

I wanted to argue with him, but I knew that would be selfish and even childish. I swallowed my frustration and sat down between Lacey and Farrah on the large blanket they had stretched over the arid ground.

With a huff, I lay down with my head over my bag and forced my eyes closed.

"Ariella." I blinked and saw Lacey touching my arm. "Time to go."

"What?" I sat up, alarmed. I glanced at my phone—no reception here, but it still had plenty of battery—and sure enough, it was eight hours later.

I jumped to my feet, appalled that I had blacked out. Around me, everyone packed their blankets and ate breakfast.

In less than five minutes, I had eaten and was ready to go.

It was a little lighter now, and I could actually see the burn marks on the ground and edges of the cliff Rage had talked about. It was like a big, fiery boulder had rolled down the ground and fallen over the cliff.

Following its trail, I glanced past the edge. "How are we getting down?"

"You shouldn't fly down," Rage said as he reached for something in his bag. "I've seen demons attack other demons in the sky. If you go out there and are attacked, we won't get to you in time."

"Good point," I muttered.

He patted the coils of ropes tied to the outside of his bag. "We'll go down with this. But first ..." He looked at Jasmin.

She stepped forward to the cliff's edge and picked up something from the pocket of her pants. It was a black rectangle, as long and thick as her index finger.

The princess noticed everyone watching her. "A master key," she said before pushing the rectangle into empty space and turning it. She let it go and the rectangle stayed in place, as if it floated on air.

Dark light shone from its surface, and a resounding click echoed around us. The air around the cliff's edge shimmered for a moment, and then everything went still.

"What was that?" Lacey asked.

"A barrier," Jasmin answered. "We don't know if it was originally here, or who put it, but so far, we have found that every truly dangerous corner has a barrier like that. And only this key can open it." She pocketed the rectangle again.

Rage put the bag down and reached for the ropes.

"We're not going down like that," Farrah said. She stepped to the cliff's edge and swept her hands forward. A thin staircase of ice started forming before her, the first step right at her feet, and the others winding down along the side of the cliff.

"Won't it melt?" Jasmin asked.

"Not while I'm holding my magic," Farrah explained.

"Thank you, Farrah," Drake said, walking to the staircase. He paused at the edge, though, and gestured to the team leader. "After you, Rage."

Rage also thanked Farrah and started down the stairs. Drake was next, then Princess Jasmin. Frank, Cyran, Barn, and Mill went right after her.

Zad stopped beside the staircase and gestured for us to go. "Ladies first."

Lacey went first, then me, and Farrah waited for Wyatt. Zad was last.

Surprisingly, the stairs were wider than they looked, and less slippery. I felt the need to hold on to a rail, but we all had good reflexes, and if someone did fall, I wouldn't hesitate to call my wings and jump after them. I knew Zad would do the same.

The staircase went on and on and on, and even though I knew it was the tension talking; it felt like we had been going down for hours.

Then finally, we reached the mist.

"Here we go," Rage called from the front. He pulled out a spear from its sheath behind his back. "Be ready for anything."

He took a few more steps and disappeared into the mist. One by one, we were swallowed by the vapor. When it was my turn, I inhaled sharply as my feet touched the gray substances. A coldness surrounded my toes and spread up as I went down. Before it reached my neck, I held my breath.

Then I was in the mist.

The stairs disappeared, the ground felt firm but I couldn't see it, I couldn't see anything but the mist.

"Lacey? Farrah?" I called.

Nothing. No answer.

Oh, shit.

I called my magic, and after a little resistance, cast a light bolt over my open palm. It only illuminated the mist and didn't show me anything.

For a second, I wondered if I should stay put or look for my friends.

Something zoomed past my back, and with a gasp, I turned toward it, but all I could see was mist, now with a golden glow because of my bolt.

"Drake?" I tried again. "Jasmin? Rage?"

Nothing again.

I inhaled deeply, trying to keep the panic down. If I

panicked now, then I wouldn't—and I had to think. What should I do?

Slowly, I took a step forward. Then another. Then another. The ground was still firm and hard underneath my boots, but that didn't mean I wasn't at the edge of another cliff.

I continued walking for a little while, counting the steps so I wouldn't go crazy in this mist.

A shape appeared in the mist and I stopped. But the shape didn't. Suddenly, a figure jumped into me and arms wound around my neck.

"Oh, my word, I'm so glad to see you," Lacey said, hugging me tight.

I hugged her back. "I know what you mean."

"This mist is horrible."

"I agree, but we found each other. Let's find the others."

Hand-in-hand, Lacey and I continued a slow trek through the mist. And even slower, we found our friends. First, we bumped into Zad, then Jasmin. It took a while, but we found Barn and Cyran, next was Farrah, then Drake and Wyatt, Mill, and finally Rage and Frank.

The moment we all held hands, the mist evaporated.

And a black land stretched out before us.

10

———

IT WAS A BARREN WORLD. A DARK FOREST WITH SCARCE, burned trees, with sand-like flat black ground, somehow firmer, and ... were those red eyes peeking from behind the trees?

"We're definitely not alone," Rage said, holding his spear tight. "Remember, be prepared for anything."

We dropped each other's hands, but no one else reached for weapons, as we all fought with magic. And in Wyatt's case, his wolf self.

To be honest, this place didn't look much different from the top of the cliff, and the terrain we had been traveling through earlier—everything dry, dead, and black. But down here, the air felt heavier, it *felt* darker and vicious.

I considered myself brave, but if I hadn't come with my friends, I wasn't so sure I would be able to continue.

"What now?" Lacey asked.

"We keep moving," Rage said. He glanced at Barn and Mill and pointed to eleven o'clock. "That direction?"

"Yes," both of them answered.

Spear in hand, Rage marched ahead and we followed. I tried keeping a leash on my magic, but it didn't want me to. At least I knew I could summon my Celestial sword in a second if needed.

As we walked among the dead trees, the creatures that had been hiding behind them moved away, to more distant trees, but they kept on spying on us. I kind of expected an attack from them, but after an hour of walking, I decided they were more afraid of us than we were afraid of them.

For that hour, barely anyone talked. All we could hear were our footsteps on the ground, the snapping of dried branches when we stepped on them, and our breathing. Everyone here was tense and their breathing elevated.

Another hour or so went by and slowly the scenery changed. The dried, dead trees became increasingly sparse, until at some point, there were barely any left. Small inclines started shaping the ground, but we stopped when we were faced with an actual valley.

We paused at the edge, right where the ground sloped down. The valley was wide and long, but it didn't look deep.

"We should go around," Mill said.

Rage gestured to the length of the valley. "It'll cost us hours." He looked down at the valley. "Let's cross it."

He was the first to jump in, followed by Drake, Jasmin, and Zad.

Wyatt and Farrah walked down, their feet skidding on the loose pebbles over the dry terrain. The two vampires and the other demons jumped in too. Lacey shrugged at me and then started walking down the steep side of the valley.

Rage was halfway through the place when I stepped in.

Instantly, the ground rumbled and fell, bringing in a cloud of dust around us. My stomach plunged up and I widened my stance, sure I would fall and be swallowed by dirt.

Then it all stopped and the dust settled.

"Everyone okay?" Drake asked, glancing around.

I looked around, checking that yes, everyone was okay, but we were in a different place. Well, it was still the same valley, but somehow it had become deeper and now the edge of the valley had become a canyon and its edge was at least thirty feet up, if not more.

"How—" The words died on my lips as dark light crackled from my left and I turned to it.

A figure knelt in the dead center of this place, his hands stretched to the sides and shackled to two short, dark pillars.

"A demon," Zad muttered.

"A higher demon," Jasmin said.

As if just now aware that he wasn't alone, the demon lifted his head, his long dark hair billowing around his sharp face. Where was the damn wind coming from?

His dark eyes zeroed in on us, his head tilting slightly. "I haven't had company in a while," he said, his voice rough, deep.

Drake took a couple of steps toward the demon but stopped at a safe distance. "Who are you?"

"Wouldn't you like to know." The edge of the demon's hard lips curved up.

"Why are you here?" Jasmin asked. She glanced back at us and whispered, "I had no idea we had a higher demon imprisoned here."

"Did you see a fireball falling from the sky?" I asked. That was the only question that interested me.

"I'll answer all of your questions," he said, the curve along his lips increasing. "If you free me."

"No," Rage snapped.

"If you're here, then there's a reason," Drake said.

Jasmin shook her head and turned to us. "He can't go anywhere. Let's move." She glanced at Rage and said in a deep voice, "We can come back after, with reinforcements, and find out more."

Rage dipped his chin once. "You heard the princess," he said to all of us. "Let's go."

I frowned, hating that we were wasting this opportunity to find out if he had seen any traces of Levi and Ylena, but I also got the feeling he wouldn't answer anything, no matter what we did to him.

With a sigh, I turned and started walking toward the huge, straight wall.

A yelp came from my right, where Lacey was a second ago.

I whirled on my heels and stilled.

Darkfire wrapped around Lacey's middle as she hovered in front of the demon.

He inhaled deeply as he sucked her magic into his through the darkfire connecting them both.

"He has magic!" Farrah shouted.

"And now he'll have more," Wyatt said with a snarl.

"Let her go!" I yelled, calling my magic. As usual, it flickered, but didn't answer. All right, sword it was. I extended my arm and my Celestial sword appeared in my hand.

However, before I could do anything, Rage stepped to my side, a spear of darkfire poised over his shoulder. "I've got this."

"You'll hit her," I muttered.

"No, he won't," Drake said, his gaze trained on Lacey as

she gasped, her arms outstretched beside her, her skin growing paler by the second.

Rage threw the spear and Drake zoomed with his incredible speed. He grabbed Lacey's hand and tugged as far to the side as she could while wrapped in darkfire, and Rage's spear flew toward the demon's shoulder.

At the last second, the demon twisted, somehow bending his arm and bringing the chain around his wrist up.

The spear hit the chain, breaking it.

With a wicked half-smile, the demon rose to his feet and inhaled deeply, taking more of Lacey's magic. Drake pulled and pulled her, but the darkfire didn't budge, not even when the vampire lord attacked it directly.

"He's going to kill her!" I walked closer, ready to slice him open before he broke the other set of chains.

"I don't need to kill her." He inhaled one more time and then the darkfire disappeared. Lacey fell heavily over Drake.

Ice shards, light magic, and darkfire rained in the demon's direction but all he did was create a wall of darkfire that reverberate with each assault but didn't break.

Undeterred by our attack, the demon wrapped darkfire around the chains that still connected his right arm to the pillar and tugged. It groaned but held. He closed his fists, putting more of whatever magic he still had on it, and pulled again.

This time, the chains broke.

But what he hadn't seen was Jasmin sneaking behind us all, behind him.

She reached him and placed a hand on his back.

Instantly, his shoulders slacked and he turned to her with dopey eyes.

"She's using her magic on him," Zad observed.

Her siren magic.

The one that entranced anyone in her web, made them enraptured by her, inescapable from her clutches, and dictated she had to consume souls to survive.

"I didn't know it worked on demons," Farrah whispered.

"Me neither," I noted. Especially a higher demon.

Unless he was faking it.

The demon stared at Jasmin in awe. He reached for her, grasped her arms, ran his hands up her neck, and cupped her face. It was as if he couldn't get enough of her.

And then he leaned in to her for a kiss.

No, not faking it.

Jasmin turned her face and his lips planted on her cheek. Closing her eyes, Jasmin placed a hand on his chest and inhaled. A shimmer appeared around the demon, almost like a faint glittery, dark snake.

"Is that …?" Wyatt asked, his eyes wide.

"His soul," Zad said, his voice clipped.

The demon's soul swirled around them, until it found Jasmin's parted lips. She inhaled deeply through her mouth and took his soul in.

"Delicious," the demon muttered. In a matter of seconds, he crumpled to the rough ground and Jasmin stepped back, as if he would stain her shoes if he kept on touching her. "My master will want to know about you …"

He went still.

Drake helped a dazed Lacey up, then toed the fallen demon. "Is he dead?"

The princess shook her head. "No. I took a lot, so he'll be weak for a long time." She glanced at Rage. "Probably long enough for us to come back and question him."

Rage nodded. "Right. We should find out who is he, why he's here."

"Who put him here," Jasmin said.

"And who his master is," Drake added.

I ran to Lacey while the others chained the fainted demon back to the pillars.

"Are you okay?" She nodded, but wobbled to the side, and I held her arms so she wouldn't fall.

"I'm okay," she whispered.

"How ... is your magic?"

"It's fine. It'll be fine."

"Are you sure?"

She nodded again. To me, she felt weak and dazed, and she needed rest. But we had to get out of here. I grabbed a cereal bar from my bag and handed it to her. "Here. It'll give you some energy."

She took the cereal, but her movements were sluggish as she unwrapped it and took a small bite.

When the demon was secured on the pillars once again, Jasmin started weaving a ward around him. "So he won't be able to get free until we come back."

"I can help," Lacey said. She shoved the last piece of cereal bar in her mouth and walked to Jasmin.

"You were just drained by a demon!" I argued.

"He didn't take much," she said.

I watched with hawk eyes as Lacey helped Jasmin, and they wove a fine thread of magic around the demon. Should he wake up and break the chains, he wouldn't be able to get through the ward.

At least, that was the hope.

Rage looked around us. "Let's get out of here."

11

To get out of the canyon, Farrah cast her ice stairs again. Zad and I offered to fly everyone over, one by one, but they preferred it this way. Once we stepped out of the canyon, the ground shook and it returned to what it was before: a not so gentle valley with nothing in it. And ahead of us, it went back to a flat, dry terrain for miles on end.

We went on for another hour before the landscape changed. Several yards ahead, the dry, flat ground curved down again; however, this time, we couldn't see the bottom.

"This could go on forever," Rage said, leaning at the edge and looking into the darkness below.

A half-broken black wooden bridge sat to our left.

We glanced down the cliff and at the other side. It wasn't terribly wide. Zad and I could fly over it, and maybe some of the others could jump across it, but most would have to cross the bridge.

"That bridge seems suspicious," Farrah said.

"I agree," Wyatt said.

"Maybe we should go around," Jasmin said.

"We don't know if there's a way around it." Zad pointed to the sides, where the cliff extended as far as we could see.

"We'll cross the bridge," Rage said, already heading toward it.

As usual, he went first, step by step, testing the broken structure to see how firm it was. A few times, it creaked, and once, a board broke and fell into the ravine.

One by one, we crossed the bridge. I was third to last, and I kept my wings ready to go in case I felt the wood giving away. A few spots, I thought it would, and once, it creaked so loudly, I thought the whole thing was coming down. But somehow, it held.

Barn and Zad were last.

"Everyone here?" Rage asked, looking at each one of us as if counting.

"Yes," Drake answered.

"Then let's keep going." Rage set out on his fast-paced march.

And we followed.

But ten steps later, the landscape changed again. It wasn't a large, flat expanse of dry, dead forest anymore, but a small island surrounded by a cliff.

"This is not what we saw from the other side," I said.

Just as I spoke, a zing rushed through us, and shadow walls emerged from the ground, surrounding the island.

"This is a prison," Zad said, his hands glowing with his magic.

"A prison within a prison?" Jasmin pondered.

"Another one?" Farrah said.

"The question is, for whom?" Rage said, his spear poised in front of him.

We fanned out a few steps, our backs to where the bridge had been, and everyone ready for a fight.

Laughter came from the other side of the island. I squinted but couldn't see anything. Slowly, a shape took form against the shadow wall, and the laughter became louder ... like a cackle.

The shape wobbled forward and away from the wall, and finally, we could see her better.

The woman looked disturbing. Smooth, dark skin, and full dark curls that were in desperate need of a brush. But the most disturbing feature of all was the huge wound in her chest, the empty hole where her heart should have been, and the river of blood across her ragged, white gown.

She lifted her head, most of her hair falling over her face, and she sniffed the air. "What is that smell? Hm, so many supernaturals together. Two angels, a fae, a wolf shifter, a witch, some demons, and my favorite ..." She smiled wide, half of her pearl-white teeth peeking through her hair. "A DuMoir vampire."

We all glanced at Drake.

His hands were tight fists, and his jaw could cut glass. "Sarki."

"You know her?" I asked, confused.

"Know me?" Sarki stopped far from us and cackled again. "His lover sent me here!"

"Lover?" Zad asked. "Thea?"

"Yes, that bitch," Sarki said.

"Thea killed you." Drake's jaw hardened. "You're supposed to be dead."

She tilted her head and a black eye appeared from beneath her hair. "I am dead ... and I'm not."

"That doesn't make sense," Lacey said.

Sarki fixed her eyes on her. "Doesn't it? You're a witch. The queen of a coven is usually the most powerful of all. Isn't your queen one of the most powerful witches who ever lived? If someone tries to kill her, do you think she'll die easily? And if she dies, do you think she just disappears?"

Lacey opened her mouth but closed it again.

"Are you saying you were a witch queen?" Wyatt asked.

"I don't need to be a witch queen to be the most powerful." The corner of her lips tugged up. "I just need the heart of one."

"Someone should tell her she's stuck in the underworld," Barn muttered.

A jolt of power ran through the walls surrounding the island. "Am I stuck here? I might be … for now." Sarki zeroed in on Jasmin. "I can feel your magic. You're one of the rulers here."

Jasmin stood tall, her chin lifted. "I am."

Sarki's lips stretched wide. "This will be fun."

"Hardly," Rage said, pointing his spear at her. "You'll die today. Not even the underworld will have you then."

He threw the spear.

It froze midair.

Sarki rose from the ground and floated several feet in the air. I called my magic. It refused to come. I extended my hand and called my sword … it also didn't come.

"What the …?"

My friends struggled with their abilities, struggled to move!

"Isn't this fun?" Sarki's voice echoed through the prison's shadow walls. "Newsflash: I might have been stuck down here for a few years, but I've only gotten stronger."

"Stop this!" Jasmin shouted.

The witch laughed. "Stop? No, no, no. There's more, dear princess. A lot more." She fixed her red eyes on Drake. "And it starts with you." She pointed a white finger at him. "Drake DuMoir, I curse you and your bloodline. On her birthday, your daughter will die and her power will be mine! And with that power, I'll kill you, your lover, and the entire DuMoir and Silverblood coven."

"No!" With all his might, Drake broke through her spell.

But the witch was ready. She turned Rage's spear and sent it flying toward Drake. The vampire didn't move in time, and the spear impaled his left shoulder, sending him to the ground.

With renewed energy and fury, we fought against the witch's powers. How the hell was she so powerful inside this prison?

Rage and Zad were the next ones to break.

The witch pointed her fingers at them, and they both fell on their knees as a white line snaked out of them.

"Their souls!" Farrah cried. With a yell, she moved one arm and sent several ice stakes toward Sarki.

The witch let go of Rage and Zad to defend herself. She pushed the ice stakes out of the way, except for one that zoomed past her head, nicking the top of her ear.

"Powerful little fae," Sarki drolled.

Finally breaking free, Farrah advanced on her.

Just to end up on her knees like the others.

"You bitch," Wyatt snarled, his eyes turning into his wolf's, on the verge of shifting, but the witch's magic wasn't letting him.

I screamed and pushed through the magic enveloping me. A second later, Lacey broke free too. We rushed the witch, but she flicked her hand and we joined the others, kneeling in front of her.

How the hell was she doing this?

I reached for my magic, and begged it to work with me here. But it was even deeper than usual, and I understood why.

I felt it.

A faint, foreign power inside me, like a string through my skin into my gut, using my magic against me.

"She's using our magic," I said, straining to get even my words out. "That's how she's so powerful."

"Ah, isn't that a great trick?" Sarki said, sounding way too cheerful. "Please, let me borrow a little more." This time, the pull was stronger and all of us groaned as she took our magic, the power that made us supernaturals, and converged them into one black, shadowy bolt between her hands. The bolt grew and grew as she got more of our magic. "And now more of yours." She glanced at Jasmin and the princess gasped, her body trembling as the witch took her power.

The bolt crackled and sizzled, and when it was bigger than her torso, Sarki flung it to the wall.

The wall crackled and sizzled.

And fell away.

"No!" Rage shouted.

Sarki cackled once more. "I'll see you all on the other side."

She half floated, half walked past us, and crossed the bridge. We fought against her immense power. She disappeared into the horizon, going back the way we came, and we remained planted in our spots. It took another fifteen minutes or so for us to finally break free.

We rushed to Drake, who was still on the ground, the

spear through his shoulder and the blade deep into the dry dirt. He was awake, but having trouble holding on to consciousness.

Lacey crouched beside him. "We need to take the spear out."

Zad produced his Celestial Sword and cut the spear close to Drake's chest. Then he and Rage held Drake's shoulders. Wyatt, Frank, and Cyran grabbed his legs. They quickly lifted him up and Drake cried as the spear left his body.

The men put him down again, and Lacey leaned over him, starting to heal him. To help, Farrah applied ice on the other side of the wound, trying to stop the bleeding.

"He won't die," Frank reminded us. "But he needs to heal."

For a moment, I forgot it wasn't easy to kill a vampire. But with that curse and the witch loose, Drake needed to regain his strength.

"I'm fine, I'm fine," Drake said, trying to get rid of Lacey halfway through the healing.

"I'm not done yet." She pushed him back and pressed her hands to his wound.

He groaned, but he let Lacey do her thing.

"What do you want to do, my lord?" Cyran asked.

He looked at me. "I'm going back to DuMoir Castle."

I nodded, not expecting anything less. If this wasn't my mission, I would have gone with him.

"You should stay and help Ariella," he said to his vampires.

"No, it's fine," I said. "You two go with Drake. Lacey might have healed him, but he might be weak for a while longer. Make sure he gets to DuMoir Castle safely."

They both nodded at me.

Lacey leaned back. "It's done."

"Thank you." Drake sat up and rolled his shoulder. He groaned. "I'll make a pit stop to see Tanner. He needs to know that crazy witch is loose in the underworld and probably looking to escape."

"No, you go directly to a portal," Jasmin said. "I'll warn Tanner and start a search party. She's not leaving the underworld." She looked at me. "Unless you need me here."

I shook my head. It was my fault we were here. It was my fault Sarki was now on the loose and had cast a curse on Aurora. My stomach clenched painfully with that knowledge.

"Go," I said. "Do what you can to stop her."

No one wasted time. Once Drake was able to stand up, he gave me one more apologetic look and left with Frank and Cyran. Jasmin went with them, at least until they reached the entrance to this section of the underworld.

Now it was Rage, Zad, Farrah, Wyatt, Lacey, Mill, Barn, and me.

"Everyone else okay?" Rage asked, looking at each one of us.

A couple of us said yes and others nodded. I was okay, only still a little shocked with what had happened. It had been crazy, fast, and intense. I hoped Jasmin and Drake caught up with that witch before she reached DuMoir Castle and did more damage.

Rage stored his spear on his back and turned to the bridge. "Then we should keep moving."

12

———

WE KEPT MOVING DEEPER INTO THE UNDERWORLD FOR A LONG time without any other issues. To be honest, I thought it was oddly quiet and kept expecting something awful at any moment.

But nothing happened.

And that only made me worry we would bump into another prisoner with great powers, and who knew what this one would do?

We walked the entire day—per our watches and phones —and didn't find anything else, no one else. When it was late, we stopped in a large desert area with only a handful of broken, burned tree trunks around us.

Rage made a small bonfire to give us more light. We sat down around the fire and ate our protein bars and drank our water. I counted how many more bars I had. If I ate only when necessary, I would have enough for a week.

It had been two days already. That left another two to go, maybe three if I rationed a little more, before we had to turn back. A sense of despair filled my chest. Would that be enough? If the past two days was any indication, it wouldn't.

But it had to be. It needed to be.

We ate in silence, everyone lost in their thoughts and stealing glances at the dark horizon. Yes, we were in a wide-open expanse of dry land, but it was dark, and some creatures could sneak up on us undetected.

After we finished eating, Rage divided us in three groups to keep watch while the others rested.

I was in the second group along with Lacey. I lay down with my bag as a pillow, but it was hard to disconnect, close my eyes, and sleep.

I tossed and turned a little, but eventually I fell asleep.

A whistling sound echoed through camp and I woke up with a start, reaching for my magic, only to be frustrated when it didn't answer.

"It's okay," Rage said.

I looked at him—he was seated in front of the dying fire, almost in the same position he had been in when we were eating, his spear resting over his folded legs.

The whistling sound came again and this time I saw it— thin, dark figures running through the sky, like deflating balloons zipping past overhead.

"What are those?"

"Some kind of spirits," he said. "Naughty, but not evil. They like to scare, but they can't do anything."

"Have you seen them before?"

He nodded. "They are all over the underworld."

The sound echoed again, fainter this time, more distant.

How could one sleep like that?

I glanced at my phone—I had slept for a little over an hour, but I suddenly felt too awake to even try again.

"You should try to go back to sleep," Rage said, echoing my thoughts.

"I will, but probably after my shift."

He nodded and looked over my shoulder. I followed his line of sight and saw Mill walking a wide perimeter of the camp.

Deciding it was a promising idea to stretch my legs, I went to the other side and circled around the camp, walking slowly and trying to keep my mind blank. But it was hard when we were in the underworld, at the bottom of a cliff, and at any moment, I expected either to have an evil being attack us, or to bump into Levi.

After a full lap, where I passed Mill, I decided patrolling the perimeter wasn't my thing and sat down across the fire from Rage.

He was still as a statue, but his eyes kept scanning the horizon.

"How did you come to work with King Tanner and Princess Jasmin?" I asked, because why not? I had nothing better to do.

He grabbed a stick and poked the fire. "It was nothing special. I had been reassigned to a European outpost, but I didn't want to go. Then I heard King Tanner was trying to assemble a team of hunters to work exclusively with him."

"Didn't Alain Heyward have a tantrum?"

As far as I knew, Alain was sort of the head of the Blackthorn Hunters, watched closely by Rey Lowe and Erin Belmont, of course.

"He went directly to Rey to complain about it, but Rey told him he thought it was a good idea, and even put out an official call for it," Rage explained. "Though, King Tanner reserves the right of approving anyone who wants to join."

I frowned. "How many hunters are there in this taskforce."

Rage scratched behind his neck. "Well, only me so far. About a handful approached the king, but he passed on them, saying they weren't right for the job."

Not right for the job? What did Tanner want in a demon hunter? Besides what they already were?

I wouldn't ever understand the mind of any ruler.

We remained quiet for the rest of the night, until it was time to switch. Rage bid me good night and went to his sleeping bag as Lacey woke up and sat down beside me.

"So, any gossip you want to talk about?"

I smiled at her. At least I could spend a few hours with my friend.

NEXT DAY, I was getting bored of walking. At some point, I kind of wished a lesser demon would attack us to have something to do.

We stopped at noon for a quick lunch and resumed walking. Thankfully, the terrain changed soon after.

A gentle incline started several yards in front of us and went on forever. We paused at the start of the incline, admiring the landscape we were about to brave—gentle ups and downs of dry ground and huge rock formations. Some were thin and pointy, others were massive and almost too smooth.

And the first thing that came to my mind was that it was the ideal place for evil beings and little naughty creatures to hide. We might not have had any action in a while, but maybe that was about to change.

"We're still on the right track?" Rage asked Barn and Mill. The demons nodded and pointed straight ahead.

This was probably bad of me, but for a moment, I couldn't help but wonder if these demons were taking us into a trap. Had they really converted and now worked for King Tanner, or were they trying to trick him? Trick us?

There was only one way to know. "Let's go," I said, gesturing for Rage to keep moving. I would have taken the lead, but I knew he wouldn't like that.

I really didn't care. I could be dead last in line, as long as we kept going.

Slowly, carefully, we went down the slope and started trekking among the rocks. Now that we were beside them, I could see that there were no small rock formations. They were all at least twice my height, and some ... I didn't even know, maybe ten times? It was dizzying to look up.

The terrain wasn't smooth here, and with the rough terrain, we tired faster. For hours, we walked this maze of rocks and sand, and I hoped Rage knew the direction we were going.

As we walked, a faint pain started inside my chest and my breathing grew slightly shallow. Was I getting winded and tired from walking so much? Angels didn't have heart attacks, did they?

The pain was so faint, it was easy to focus on something else and forget it. If it increased, I would ask Lacey to take a look at me. With her healing abilities, I was sure she could help me, whatever it was.

We stopped a few times to rest and eat and drink, but for the most part, we trudged on. I couldn't help feeling frustrated again at how slow we were going.

This was taking way too long, but what other option did we have?

"Look." Farrah pointed up to a tall, narrow rock formation.

It seemed like the tip had been broken and the top was smudged in black.

"The fireball," I muttered.

Ignoring the increasing pain in my chest, I followed the path I thought the fireball had fallen, and I could barely contain myself and my racing heart as I saw more clues: broken rocks, black marks on the rock sides, a faint burnt scent in the air, and finally a huge, black crater that had flattened the terrain and exploded a couple of rocks to dust.

I froze, my eyes huge as I stared at the crater.

If it hadn't been Levi and Ylena, then what was it? Meteors in the underworld? I doubted that was a thing.

"This is certainly where the fireball landed," Rage said.

Farrah turned to Lacey. "Can't you sense your brother's aura or something?"

"I can try," Lacey said.

The pain in my chest increased and I realized it wasn't pain. It was a forceful tug. "The bond," I whispered. I pressed a hand to my chest and almost wept for joy. "I can feel the bond."

Lacey stared at me with huge eyes. "That means he's here. That he's close."

My chest squeezed and the tug almost made me breathless. I walked into the crater, approached the center, looked around, but saw no one, no clues of where he might have gone.

Lacey followed me. She crouched down in the center of the crater and touched the darkened, burned ground. "I can sense it … him. And someone else." She looked up at me. "He was here."

"Levi!" I called out.

Wyatt sniffed the air. "I think I got a hint of their scent, but it's faint. If that's them, then they aren't here anymore."

"Can you follow the scent?" I asked, full of hope.

"I can try." Wyatt started taking off his clothes, and all of us turned around. Except for Farrah. "My senses are stronger when shifted."

I heard a groan and a couple of seconds later, a little whine. We turned and saw Wyatt in his wolf form—a big, deadly creature with brown fur and sharp teeth.

He started prowling, smelling the crater. He looked like an ant lost in a maze. I was about to deem this a failure, when he walked to the edge of the crater, sniffed the air, and let out a short yelp.

"That way," Farrah said.

We rushed after Wyatt as he left the crater and weaved a path among the rocks. A couple of times, he circled around, doubled over, went back a few yards … and I did my best not to get frustrated.

The pain inside my chest now turned into a faint tug that was almost in sync with my fast-beating heart.

All this time, I had tried not to think about Levi much. I didn't want to remember our moments together, especially what he had said right before disappearing through the portal.

But now that we were getting closer to him—I hoped— the emotions I had fought so hard wanted attention. The moment I saw him I didn't know what I would do. Punch him hard for what he did or hug him tight and never let him go.

Because I truly didn't want to let him go, and that scared me like hell.

It was crazy how everything could change in a matter of days.

I don't know how long we zigzagged between the rocks, but I could feel the tug becoming stronger the farther into the territory we went.

Just when a deep tug took my breath away, Wyatt stopped between two big rocks and howled.

We rushed to his side.

Beyond the rocks was a large clearing, where lots of other rocks had been before, but now were broken into little pieces. Some were dust on the ground.

"What the—?" The question died on my lips as a black bolt zipped through the air and hit one of the rock formations across the clearing. The bolt caused the rock to shake and several broken pieces fell to the ground.

"That's what happened," Zad said.

But I was still shocked to see a black bolt.

Which meant ...

With a shriek, Ylena zoomed through the clearing. Another bolt came from the left and missed her by a hair. She hissed and flew a little higher, hopping over a rock formation.

And we all gawked at her.

"Is that her?" Farrah asked.

Lost for words, I nodded.

Yes, it was Ylena.

But it wasn't.

Her blond hair was longer, wilder, her clothes were in tatters, she had a craze glint in her eyes, and a snarl on her lips. Her skin was grayish, and her hands ... her fingertips had become black and razor sharp, like claws.

But the most shocking of all was her wings: they were now black.

Like Zad's and mine.

"That's what happens when you spend time locked in the underworld," Zad said, his voice low. Sad. "You go insane, and if you're an angel, your wings turn black."

"Did Levi go insane too?" Lacey asked, glancing to where the bolt had come from a moment ago.

I also wanted to know that.

As if answering her question, he walked into the clearing and I couldn't control my reaction. I gasped as the tug turned violent and my heart squeezed.

Levi was here in his demon form.

But he was different. He was larger, his horns were longer, and his skin was darker than before. His wings ... they were at least twice their normal size.

He had the same crazed glint in his eyes as Ylena's, but he wasn't snarling. He was growling like an animal ready for dinner.

Levi stopped a few yards later and sent another bolt of darkfire at Ylena. She snickered, flapped her wings, twisted in midair, and landed atop the rock again.

"That's the best you can do?" she said, her voice shrill like a ghost's.

With a growl, Levi cast another bolt.

We stood several yards to their side, at the edge of the clearing, but they were unaware of our presence.

"Keep Ylena busy," I said before dashing into the clearing. "Levi!"

Slowly, Levi let the bolt fade and turned to me. His bright

red eyes met mine and for a second, I wanted to cry with relief. He saw me! I was here! He would be fine now.

His lips curled back and he snarled.

With a flap of his powerful wings, Levi lunged at me, his hands in front of him, ready to strike.

I froze.

Someone rammed into me from the side, knocking me to the ground as Levi zoomed past me, his claws an inch from my head.

I fell hard, hurting my shoulder with the impact, and Lacey landed on top of me.

"What?" I blinked, as if waking from a daze.

"He's not himself." Lacey stood and offered her hand to me.

I grasped it and helped her pull me up, just as Levi whipped around in the air and came at us again.

"I don't want to fight him," I said.

"Me neither." She cast a barrier in front of Levi. He slammed into it and fell to the ground.

A scream came from our left and I couldn't help looking —the others attacked Ylena, but she sent a light bolt to shock them all and flew away.

Levi stood, punching the barrier, which broke and faded in the air. He growled at us. "Stay out of this," he said, his voice guttural. A monster's.

He leapt into the air and flew after Ylena.

What the hell had happened?

13

"Come on." I started walking in the direction they had gone. "We gotta keep moving."

"Ariella, wait," Farrah said.

"We can't wait. If we wait, they might get too far." With those wings, they just might. I glanced at Zad. "You and I can go after them, get to them faster."

"But Rage said it's not a good idea to fly here," Zad said.

I gestured to the horizon. "It seems to be working fine for them!"

"Ariella," Rage said, his voice firm, commanding.

"What?" I snapped, though I refused to look at him. At them.

Because I knew what was coming, I knew what they would say, and I hated to admit I understood. I even agreed. But that didn't make this easy.

They stood there, forming a half circle around me, waiting for me to calm down. Only Barn and Mill weren't so close, their attention on the surroundings, watching for unexpected enemies.

I let out a long breath and faced them. "I can't pretend I didn't see him."

"No one is asking you to do that," Farrah said, her tone too calm. "But we've been through many difficult situations and you know that sometimes, we need to take a step back and assess the factors."

I groaned and looked at Lacey. "Don't you want to go after your brother?"

"You know I do." She sounded almost hurt. "But I don't think he was himself. If he was, then he wouldn't have attacked us. Attacked you."

"He was a full-fledged demon," Wyatt said. He had shifted back after Levi and Ylena left, and put on pants.

"It felt like he forgot who he is," Lacey continued. "When we were researching the underworld, I remember reading about how some areas can mess with someone's head. Even if you spend a brief time there, it can literally make you insane."

"I was in a place like that." Zad nodded. "My friends couldn't handle it and died. It took everything to stay sane, and honestly, I don't think I'm the same." He inhaled. "To this day, I still have nightmares about it."

He had been betrayed by someone on his squad and they all ended up in the underworld by mistake. But they had been in a prison like this, without any means of leaving, and slowly they went crazy and died.

Zad had said that had been the worst part—holding on to his mind while watching everyone he knew succumb to this place.

"Perhaps this is one of those sites," Farrah said.

"Which means, we're going insane too?" Wyatt asked.

"We've been here for two days," Rage said. "Besides, we're together and we have a purpose. It would take a lot more to make us insane."

"Unless we get stuck here for twenty years," Zad said, going for a joke.

I glared at him. Not a suitable time for jokes!

"I can see that," Lacey said, her voice low. "Levi had a lot of rage in his heart, his demon side always spoke loudly. He came here, what, one week ago? Ten days? And was alone with the person he hates most. That would drive anyone insane."

"He's not insane," I snapped. "He's lost in his demon. We need to find him and bring him back."

"Do you think you can?" Farrah asked.

I stared at her. "If it was Wyatt, do you think you could?"

She looked at Wyatt and nodded.

I realized what I had said. I had compared the true fated mates bond Wyatt and Farrah shared, to what Levi and I had. That my feelings for him were probably like Farrah's for Wyatt.

Could they be?

I didn't want to dwell on it. "So, what are your orders, Rage?"

"We go after them, carefully, and observe from a distance," the mission leader said.

"And then?" Lacey asked. I knew that deep inside she was as anxious as I was. She was better at controlling herself.

"I'm not sure," Rage admitted. "We might need to separate the two of them somehow, so we can get to Levi without Ylena drawing his attention."

"And then?" It was Farrah this time.

"I'll talk to him," I said, feeling a little nervous about that. If *talking* with him would do the trick, then maybe he would have hesitated when he saw me.

I was probably overthinking this. I was overthinking and overfeeling everything right now.

"Me too." Lacey reached over and held my hand in hers. "I'll spell him, if I have to."

I squeezed her hand, grateful for having her in my corner.

"All right," Rage said. "You two deal with Levi, the rest of us will keep Ylena busy. Understood?"

We all nodded and said yes.

I FELT like all we did the past couple of days was walk. This time, it wasn't a long trek, but because I had seen Levi and knew we were close, it felt like an eternity.

With each step, the tug in my chest increased, the bond teasing me that we were closer.

After an hour, I started getting nervous. Maybe I should fly ahead. Zad could go with me. But I knew they wouldn't approve of my plan, and I wasn't sure I could hold myself back from him.

"If we don't find them in the next hour, we'll stop to rest," Rage announced.

Stopping to rest would only put us farther behind them. The irritation and the anxiety were talking louder now, making me feel like a petulant child.

I hated it.

I hated this.

I wanted to find him right now.

Walking to my side, Lacey slipped her hand in mine again. "I know this is hard for you. It's hard for me too."

I held her grip. "It's torture."

She nodded. "But we'll find him, we'll find a way to get through to him, and we'll leave with him."

With Levi.

Which brought something else to mind. "What will we do with Ylena?"

"You tell us," Rage said.

I frowned. "I don't know. The right answer would be to kill her."

"But it's not that easy," Farrah said.

I knew she meant it wasn't easy for me.

It wouldn't be easy to kill her even if she was a stranger. She was the most powerful archangel ever, the oldest one.

"We'll cross that bridge when we get there," Lacey said.

I nodded, thankful they understood the conflict inside me. "As much as I think Elysium would be safer with her gone, Ylena was the mastermind of this whole thing." I was grasping for another angle. "She has answers we need. That's the only way to undo the damage she's already inflicted."

"True," Zad said. "We need her alive."

Imprisoning her would be hard, but one thing at a time.

First, we needed to find them.

A shriek echoed from the sky and in a fast swoop, Ylena flew to us.

She crashed into me, almost driving me to the ground, but she closed her arms around my waist and carried me away.

I struggled and called my magic, but my magic refused to obey. I started on my wings, but Ylena knew what I was up to.

She pressed a hand to my back and sent a jolt of magic coursing through me that made me dizzy, heavy. I could barely move my head, much less my limbs.

I looked down at my friends as they became smaller and smaller.

"Ariella, no!" Lacey shouted.

Rage prepared to send a darkfire bolt, but Farrah stopped him. "You might hit Ariella."

Zad's wings erupted from his back and launched him after us.

Ylena twisted in the air, sending a spray of light bolts at Zad. He dodged all but the last two. They hit him in a wing and in the chest.

He went down.

"No!" I cried, though the words stuck to my tongue.

With a snarl, Ylena sent another jolt of magic into me and I slumped over her shoulder.

I fought to stay conscious. If I fainted, I was afraid I might never wake up.

After I don't know how long, Ylena landed and dropped me on the rough ground like a sack of potatoes. I grunted in pain and rolled to my side, glad I was recovering my senses and movement, though too slow for my taste.

Ylena tucked her dark wings behind her back and circled me, like a bird of prey teasing its food.

Sitting up, I took in the surroundings. The rock formations were spread out, creating wider paths and clearings.

Ylena snarled at me, and I looked back at her.

"If you're going to kill me, just do it," I said, pushing to my knees. My strength trickled into my limbs.

"Who are you?" she asked in a shrill voice.

I blinked at her. "You don't know me?"

"I know you but I don't remember you." She tilted her head. "I feel strong things for you. But I don't know why."

What the hell? Had she slipped so deep into insanity? Forgotten everything? And her ashen skin, her dark fingertips turned claws? Were they a trick of this place too?

If I stayed here for a week, would I become like that too?

"Do you know who you are?" I asked.

She tilted her head to the other side, but snarled at me.

Which was my answer.

Ylena didn't remember who she was. She didn't remember me, and perhaps she didn't remember anything, which meant I could use that to my advantage. I could trap her before her curiosity ran out and she decided to attack me.

"You're Ylena," I said, standing up. A wave of dizziness coursed through me, but I blinked fast and contracted my core, willing myself to stay upright. "You were my mentor and friend."

The word felt like poison on my throat, but I was playing a role here. Nothing more.

She stared at me, as if she could feel it made sense, that it was true, but she couldn't *see* it.

"What—?"

A growl came from somewhere behind me, and I turned, only to get dizzy again and almost trip on my feet.

On a large rock formation was an opening, like the mouth of a cave.

The growl came again from there.

From behind me, Ylena closed her hand around my neck and pressed her claws into my throat. "She's here!"

I jerked, trying to disentangle myself from her, but damn, she either had gotten stronger, or she had always hidden her full strength.

I forgot all about her when the growl echoed a third time and Levi emerged from the cave.

He was still in his demon form and looking more terrifying than ever.

I stilled.

"She's all yours," Ylena said, and only now I noticed her hand was gone and she was several feet back.

"What are you doing?" I asked, my voice low.

"He seemed to take interest in you," she said. "You're my ticket to get rid of him."

"What—?"

Levi's red eyes locked on me and I stilled.

Ylena flew away and he stared at me.

I retreated.

He growled louder this time and I froze.

With deliberate steps, he advanced toward me.

I would have been so glad for finding him except for the murderous gleam in his eyes, the tension in his powerful body; it made me want to run.

"Levi, it's me," I said. "Ariella."

He stopped, huffed, and snarled. "I don't know you." His voice was so deep, so guttural, it was hard to believe it was him.

"Yes, you do. I can feel you in here." I pressed a hand to the center of my chest. "Can't you feel me too?"

His hand started up, but he closed it into a fist and lowered it again. He growled. "You're an angel. Just like her. You want to kill me too."

"No, I don't." I took a step forward but forced myself to stop. I was scared of him, and I didn't want him to think I was attacking him. "I want to help you. To bring you back. To take you away from here."

"Away." He looked up, to the dark sky.

"Would you like that?"

His eyes returned to me. "I want to kill the angel." In a flash, his wings flapped fast, pushing him to me. His hand closed around my throat and he shoved me against a rock formation. He leaned in to me and snarled. "I can kill this angel too."

"Levi, you don't want to kill me." I struggled against his hold, but he was too damn strong for me. "I'm your mate."

"Lies!" he shouted. "The other angel lied to me. You lie to me. Trick me. Trap me."

I stared at him. He wasn't as far gone as Ylena if he could remember how we first got stuck together. "Right. I trapped you, but it worked out, right?"

He bared his teeth. "You trapped me? Now?"

Despite the situation and being slightly out of breath, I couldn't help but stare at him and hear my heart breaking. He was a giant and a brute like this, but he was also dense. His cockiness, his brightness, everything that made Levi himself was gone.

"No—"

He squeezed my throat a little more. "I'm going to kill you."

"Don't make me hurt you," I croaked, barely able to speak.

"As if you could." He brought his other hand up, his claws poised to strike.

Damn it.

I didn't have time to call my magic, so I summoned my sword instead. I turned it sideways and hit his waist with the flat side of the blade, but I hit hard, knowing he would barely feel anything.

But he let out a roar and loosened his grip.

I brought my leg up and half kicked, half pushed him back, and before he could come at me again, I twisted out of the way and ran. In five steps, I had my wings out and I soared into the air.

Of course, he came after me.

To catch me? To kill me?

I had no idea, and until we could draw the circle and trap him, I wasn't staying here to find out.

I flapped my wings fast. Three times, he almost caught me, but I was smaller, and more agile. I twisted out of the way and changed direction.

It didn't take me long to realize I had no idea where I was going. I could be going deeper into the territory, away from my friends.

That wouldn't do.

I reached deep inside me, got a firm hold on my magic, and pulled it to the surface. It was stubborn, but I had no choice here. I extended a hand up and threw sparks in all directions. They went far and exploded like fireworks.

A few seconds later, black sparks came from my left, going straight up to the sky.

There. That was Lacey.

I turned and zoomed toward them.

I didn't like bringing Levi to them, like a bomb ready to explode, but I couldn't deal with him alone.

Levi almost caught me again, his claw swiping inches from my head. He definitely planned to kill me.

When he came back to himself, would he regret it? Would he miss me?

Damn it, what was I thinking?

I pushed those thoughts away and focused on getting to my friends.

Thankfully, Lacey shot the sparks back up again a moment later and I was able to course correct and fly toward them. It would still take another two or three minutes for me to get to them.

I just hoped they were thinking what I was thinking.

To make sure they had enough time, I gritted my teeth and circled around them. I almost regretted it when Levi caught my hair and pulled me back, making me shriek in pain. I had to flap my wings hard not to fall, and I kicked him in the stomach. He held on to my hair for as long as he could, but when I summoned my sword and pushed the hilt hard under his chin, he let me go.

I almost plummeted to the ground.

The sparks exploded again, closer this time, and I assumed that was their ready signal.

I flew low and saw them in a small space between the rocks.

Large enough for a witch's circle.

I flew outside of the circle's line, but Levi was so intent on catching me, he didn't look down. He was about to fly inside the circle when a light bolt slammed into his side, pushing him back and out of the circle's range.

Levi fell to the ground several feet back, but was up a second later, his wings spread out behind him, his claws ready, his teeth bared. He looked up and sure enough, Ylena stood atop a rock, another bolt twirling in her open palm.

I landed beside Lacey and the others.

Levi snarled at Ylena and she laughed.

"A proposition," she said, her shrill voice cutting through the air.

Levi growled. "I don't make deals with you."

"But this one will get us out of here."

That actually caught his attention.

"Whatever they are doing, we need to stop them," Rage said. He got his spear and the others got ready for a fight.

As if they could read each other's mind, Levi nodded and Ylena smiled—a wicked thing that chilled me to the bone.

Looking at Levi, she raised the bolt in her hand and threw it at our feet!

We jumped back, but the impact was strong enough to make us stumble.

In a flash, she and Levi flew toward us.

I called my sword, Lacey cast her magic, Wyatt turned into his wolf ... but before we could do anything, a rain of light bolt and darkfire fell over us.

Farrah cast an ice bridge over our heads.

But that was all distraction.

Levi and Ylena swooped under the bridge. Levi caught Rage, passed him on to Ylena, and then slammed into me. He closed his strong arms around me and flew away with me.

"Let me go!" I screamed.

He snarled at me, and when I struggled against him, he tightened his hold, making it impossible for me to move.

I glanced back and saw as Zad came after us, but Ylena was ready for him. She appeared right in front of him, taking him by surprise, and threw that charged bolt right at him.

Zad grunted in pain as the shock rocked his body. He lost control and went down.

"No," I whispered, hoping he would recover enough to catch himself before hitting the ground.

Rage fought Ylena's hold, and though she was strong, it was probably hard carrying him and fighting him. Rage lost his spear and Ylena shocked him. He slumped in her arms.

I considered calling my magic and trying to surprise Levi

with it long enough for him to drop me, but then I realized that this might be a good thing. He didn't seem intent on killing me, and if he took me with them, I would know where they were going, what their plan was.

Despite my instincts, I stopped fighting.

And let Levi take me.

14

———

SOMEHOW, YLENA HAD FIGURED SOME THINGS OUT. FOR ONE, we were in a prison, and two, Rage had a key to get out of here.

She reached into his pocket and grabbed the black rectangle. She held on to it as we approached the cliff and the mist appeared. At first, it was like morning fog, but soon, it was thick and almost tangible.

For a good fifteen minutes, we flew blind.

Until the mist dissipate and we came face-to-face with the cliff wall. Ylena and Levi had to pull back with all of their might before we slammed into the wall. They pulled up and flew to the top of the cliff.

At the edge, they bumped into an invisible wall.

"Where's the lock?" Ylena asked Rage. He pressed his lips tight. "Tell us, or I'll drop you."

He glanced at me, determined to not reveal anything.

With a snarl, Ylena wrapped a hand around Rage's throat. "You." She stared me. "Tell me or I'll drop him."

Shit. "I don't know where it is."

"Liar!" She loosened her grip and Rage slipped a little. His eyes went wide for a moment.

"I seriously don't know!" I had seen Jasmin holding the key to the wall; there were no markers.

Ylena hissed. "You're useless to me." She opened her arms.

Rage fell.

"No!" I screamed, watching as he disappeared into the mist. I glared at Ylena. "What the hell happened to you?" This couldn't be the same angel who had trained me, who had been such an inspiration to me.

She didn't acknowledge me. Instead, she turned to the invisible wall and simply pushed the key into it.

The key held and Ylena turned it. A shimmer ran through the wall as it disengaged. She dropped the key at the edge of the cliff, as if it was trash, and with a wicked smile, she crossed the barrier.

Levi followed her.

A couple feet past the barrier, they landed and turned to each other. Without wasting a breath, Levi growled and threw a big bolt at Ylena. She barely dodged it, and the bolt singed her hair.

"You," she snarled. "I helped you!"

"I'm a demon," he said with a growl. "You should know better."

He prepared to send another bolt at her, but she was faster. She threw her light magic at us. Levi's grip loosened around me and I jumped away from him—and landed right beside the discarded key.

I wasn't sure if this would work, or if they would find it, but I grabbed the key and flung it over with a small prayer that somehow Rage had survived the fall, and that they would find the key.

With a growl, Levi surged over me, wrapped one arm around my waist and flew straight up, fast and hard, taking my breath away.

With me secured, he sent another bolt her way, and she took to the air to avoid it.

Then Levi zipped away from her.

I frowned, watching as he kept throwing bolts Ylena's way, until all the dodging made her lose steam, and she was left behind.

Why was he doing that?

Then it hit me. Levi knew certain parts of the underworld, probably the castle and the main entrance and he didn't want Ylena to follow him.

When Levi emerged past a tall mountain that looked like a strategic wall and into the river of lava, I knew I was right.

And somehow, King Tanner had been prepared for this as at least two dozen demon hunters stood at the bridge.

Levi flew up, toward the infinite-looking ceiling, avoiding any of the hunters and their strikes.

He arced around the castle and went to the gates, which were also heavily guarded.

Levi sped up, and when we were close enough to be hit by the demon hunters, he draped his wings around us like a shield and barreled into the last line of defense, taking a couple of hunters with us as we crossed the portal into the human realm.

On the other side, the demon hunters tried striking him, but Levi didn't stop. He didn't even slow down as he opened his wings, flew higher, and disappeared into the sky, taking me with him.

I instantly recognized the gate we had come through, near Winnipeg. Once we left the gate's grounds, the glamour went up and we flew past the fake farmhouse.

The sky was stained orange and blue and purple as the sun set to our right, which told me we were going south. The ground was covered in fresh snow and it was freezing. I had a thin leather jacket, but it wasn't enough for this cold.

Though he seemed more demon than human right now, Levi was smart. He flew fast and far from the underworld entrance. We were following the twisting flow of the Red River, which went on for hundreds of miles. At some point, I was sure we had crossed into the United States.

He held me tight the entire time, and only glanced at me once or twice. I knew he wouldn't let me fall, but I still grasped his arms as tight as I could. However, after hours flying, I didn't have any strength to hold on anymore and slumped against him.

I looked up at his menacing, yet handsome face. He looked more monster than anything else like this, but I could see the traces of his human form underneath it all.

I placed a hand on his chest, feeling the fast beat of his heart. I had to believe he was still the same underneath the monster, and somehow, I would get to him.

When the sun was gone, Levi veered inland, taking us from the river route, and deep into the woods. He stopped in some hills and found a cave—just a wide overhang under the trees where we could hide for the night.

He dropped me inside the cave and stepped back. Knowing I couldn't run from him—and honestly, not sure I wanted to—I sat on the cold, hard ground and hugged my legs.

There was no snow here but it was still too cold.

Levi frowned and snarled at me. "Don't run."

I didn't dignify his command with an answer.

He disappeared for a good ten minutes.

I did consider running, but what then? If I wanted to reach past his demon self, I had to stay with him.

So, I patiently and coldly waited for him.

Levi came back with an armful of firewood. He deposited it at the mouth of the cave and sent a spark of darkfire to them. The wood caught on fire instantly.

I scooted closer to the fire, my palms out. "Aren't you going to sit?"

"I'm not cold," he said and I almost winced, still not used to hearing his demon voice.

But he had noticed I was cold. He had made the fire for me. He might not understand it yet, but he cared. I needed to use that.

"I know, but I am. If you sit next to me, it'll help." I was pushing it.

He huffed and didn't oblige. He stood on the other side of the fire, tall and regal, ready for a battle. In the distance, an owl hooted and a branch cracked.

His body tensed.

"Relax," I said. "It's just an animal."

"They can attack."

"Oh, I doubt they will get too close."

Levi was the most dangerous animal in these woods, I was sure.

I felt my stomach contract with hunger. When was the last time I had eaten? I had no idea where my bag was. I had probably dropped it somewhere in the underworld, before this whole ordeal started.

Levi paced in front of the fire while I trembled with each faint, chill breeze that blew our way.

I was giving him some time to calm down and be bored before I struck.

Finally, when he paused and looked up at the bare trees, I found my opening.

"What's your plan?" I asked. He looked at me. "What will you do now? Just stay here with me? Let me die of cold and hunger? Start a war? What?"

His brows curled down. "I want my revenge."

"Revenge. Against what? Who?"

"My enemy."

"Ylena? The angel who was in the underworld with you?" He grunted as if to answer yes. "Why do you want revenge against her?"

His frown deepened.

He didn't know. Levi had been so lost to the monster, he didn't know why he had been fighting her in the first place.

"Why did you take me?" I tried another approach.

The demon stared at me, his eyes dark, intense. "I don't know."

"That's not a good answer." I pressed a hand to my chest. "Did you feel something here?"

He glanced down at my hand and averted his eyes. He did! That had to be it. Feeling confident about this, I stood, walking around the fire and closer to him. His gaze was fixed on me the entire time, and his body tensed as I approached him.

I halted a foot from him and placed my hand on his chest again, like I had done when we were flying, but this time, nothing else was distracting him.

"We're bonded," I told him. "You're tied to me and I'm tied

to you. We feel each other. We have feelings for each other." I leaned in closer. "You like me."

With a growl, Levi caught my arms and pushed me against the closest tree, its trunk wide and hard on my back. He bared his teeth right in my face.

"There are no feelings." His voice was even deeper now, rougher, chillier. I went rigid, afraid I had pushed him too far too fast. "I don't feel anything. I just want my revenge and you're standing in my way."

He snapped his sharp teeth and punched the tree right above my head. The trunk creaked and cracked with his strength, but it didn't break.

I paled.

"You're nothing to me," he said with a snarl.

He turned his back to me and pushed up, flying away.

I slumped against the tree, breathing hard.

Shit, what had I done?

As the night became darker and colder, I did consider leaving. But to go where? I had no idea where I was, which direction I could go. I didn't have my phone to reach anyone or look at the GPS, and I could hear animals prowling nearby.

I could fly up, try to see something in the distance, but in this darkness?

It was better if for now if I stayed with the dying fire. I did get up at some point, to use the "restroom" and find more firewood, but I never went far, afraid of getting lost or being taken by surprise by the animals.

It didn't take long for me to get sleepy, even though I was

freezing and starving. I lay down beside the small fire, as close as I could get without getting burned, hugged myself, and closed my eyes.

When I woke up, it was still dark, but I wasn't shivering anymore. Levi lay beside me, his body an inch from mine, and his wings covering us both. It was like a cocoon of warmth, like a cozy blanket.

I glanced up at him, but in the near darkness, it was almost impossible to see anything. Still, I stared at his face, and I knew that underneath the demon, underneath this evilness that had overtaken him, he was still the same.

The one who cared for me, even though he shouldn't. Even though he really didn't want to.

And that gave me hope.

I stayed as quiet as I could, watching him as he slept. His chest moved up and down. I wondered, was this the first time he had truly slept since he disappeared with Ylena?

My heart squeezed—half pain for him, half the bond pulling me toward him.

I rolled to my right side, tucked my right arm underneath my head, and faced him fully. I let my left hand hover over his stonelike chest, not really touching, but close. My fingertips brushed against something on his waist and I paused. Gently touching my fingers to his side, I realized what it was.

I brought my fingers to my line of sight.

Blood.

I sat up, pushing his wings from above me.

Levi groaned, but besides stirring a little, he didn't wake up. Frowning, I scooted closer to him and saw it.

A large wound on his right side, the blood dripping down his back and drenching the ground.

What?

I shook his shoulder. "Levi." He groaned but kept on sleeping. I placed a hand on his forehead. He was burning up. "Shit," I muttered as my heart squeezed.

I stared at the wound. Why wasn't it healing? Or was it healing slowly? If it stayed open for long, it would get infected. But I had nothing with me. My bag was gone, and I didn't even have my phone to call for help.

I leaned into him. "Levi," I called again, but apparently, he was too far gone with the fever to realize what was going on. A demon this big, this powerful … this wound had to be deep and wreaked havoc on the inside to have him knocked him out like this.

I hovered a hand over the wound and lowered it again. There were angels who could use their magic to heal, but I had never mastered that when I could use my magic. Now that it was all messed up, I couldn't risk doing more damage.

But I couldn't let him stay like this either.

I shot to my feet and created a plan in my head. I would fly out and—

An unnatural heap caught my sight and I did a double take. Was that a mound of mountain lions? My mouth opened as I realized they were dead, with blood smeared all over them. I followed the trail of blood, and found it actually started a few feet from where I was.

Wait.

I gaped at Levi's feverish demon form. I had been alone last night. Or had I? Had Levi been close the entire time? And when mountain lions got too close to me while I slept, he killed them all?

My heart tugged.

I took off my jacket, held on to it, released my wings, and took to the skies.

15

I SOARED HIGH, SO I COULD SEE AS FAR AS THE FOREST ALLOWED me. But there was only green everywhere I looked.

I had to fly around a little, until finally, I spotted a town in the distance, along the Red River's bank to the south. I flew low and directly to it. When I was close, I dove into the trees.

I landed outside of town, in a wooded area, and I put on my jacket to hide the holes in my shirt.

Since I had no money on me, I found an ATM at a gas station, shocked it with my magic, and withdrew a nice sum.

I felt bad about stealing, and I made a mental note to atone for my sins after this whole ordeal was done.

If it ever was done.

With cash in my pocket, I went into the local pharmacy and bought a little of everything—ibuprofen, gauze, tape, Neosporin, and even needle and thread. I also bought a bottle of water, and those reusable totes so I could carry it all.

The lady behind the counter watched me, not hiding her suspicion. She tried talking to me, asking me where I was from, when I got into town, where I was staying, why I was here, and more.

"I'm just passing through," was all I said.

I did see her cell phone tucked into the pocket of her apron and thought about asking to borrow it. I could call Thea. They would come, take Levi, lock him in a cell, and treat him like a criminal, at least until I was able to bring him back.

And he was hurt. I knew they could heal him with magic, but for some reason, I didn't want to share this. I didn't want to share him. Not yet.

Beside the pharmacy was a bakery. I couldn't resist stopping there and grabbing a couple of croissants, donuts, and muffins. I was starving and Levi would be too, once he healed. I even ordered a to-go cup with coffee, though I knew it would be cold by the time I got back to Levi.

I stepped out of the bakery and almost ran into a man. Men actually.

"Hey there, doll," one of them said, smiling. He reeked of alcohol. He had a golden tooth right beside a missing one.

I glanced at the handful of men in front of me. They ranged from twenty to forty-something, and they all looked like they had spent the night out, drinking.

I stepped back, allowing them to walk in.

The golden-toothed man gestured for me. "Ladies first."

Knowing I could kick their asses if they tried anything— or at least I could spill boiling coffee on their heads—I walked past them. They kept their gazes on me the entire time.

"Need help, doll?" another one asked. This one had cropped black hair and a nasty scar on his right temple.

"No, thanks." I kept going, my steps faster and faster.

The men stood in front of the bakery, holding the door open, watching me as I put distance between us.

I turned a corner and let out a long breath, relieved those creeps were far behind now. I glanced side to side as I made my way back to the wooded area. The sun was higher now, but I flew low and held my coffee.

Thankfully, it didn't spill.

I landed beside Levi and noticed he hadn't moved an inch.

I knelt beside him and placed the bag down with all the supplies. I started working. I grabbed five tablets of Ibuprofen, placed them in his mouth and spilled a little of the water down his throat. He coughed, growled in his delirious stated, but swallowed.

Then, I used the water to clean the blood around the wound, which actually proved to not be as bad as I first thought. Once the dried blood was gone, all that was left were three long gashes across the side of his waist, which weren't too deep and had already stopped bleeding.

I frowned, wondering if I should do anything at all, but I had come so far and his healing still seemed too slow for my taste. Since he was out of it, I prepared the thread and needle and sewed the gashes closed with a handful of knots each. It definitely wasn't as neat or tight as stitches, but hopefully, they would help when his magic decided to act.

Then, I applied a great deal of Neosporin over the gashes and covered them with a thin layer of gauze and tape.

All the while, Levi groaned, hissed, and jerked a little, but he didn't wake up.

When I was done, I sat back and let my shoulders sag.

Was there any possibility of infection? Again, I tried

remembering he was a damn powerful demon and his healing should do what it had to do.

But how he got like this in the first place was beyond me.

I inhaled deeply, shook off the tension in my shoulders, and reached for the coffee. It was cold.

I held the cup with both hands, closed my eyes, and focused on my magic, finding it deep inside me, hiding and unwilling to cooperate. I teased it, coaxed it toward me, to let me reach for it. I didn't need much for this, just a sliver. The magic opened up a tiny slit and I grabbed it tight. I concentrated the light magic on my palms and heated up the cup—and my coffee. Afterward, I dropped the magic and it recoiled fast and deep inside me, almost painfully.

Ungrateful bitch.

I forgot about it and looked at my coffee—steam rose from the black liquid. Great. Trying not to think of Levi too much, I grabbed a croissant and had breakfast.

But it was impossible not to think about him.

As I ate, he whimpered and jerked, looking way too vulnerable for a demon his size.

Hopefully, soon, he wouldn't be a demon anymore. Well, not like this, at least. Soon, he would regain his memories, his feelings, and the ability to shift into his human form.

And together, we could plan on going after Ylena and saving Elysium.

I finished my croissant and my coffee, and even though I had been starving before, now I felt full and unsatisfied.

How long would it be before Levi was feeling better? What if other animals came back and my magic failed me?

Shaking my head, I stood. No, I couldn't do nothing. Whenever I tried that, my mind got away from me and I ended up in a worse place.

I needed to do something.

The dying fire behind Levi caught my attention. It was still cold—damn, I should have bought a thicker jacket when I went into town, but I was worried about a certain demon—and only angels knew how long we would stay here.

I walked the perimeter of our "camp," careful to take a wide berth past the mountain lions' bodies, and gathered firewood. I took my time since there was no rush—Levi was sleeping, I had nothing to do, and walking was exercise.

Thirty minutes later, I placed the firewood on the fire, hoping it would be enough to ignite it. But it wasn't. Like I did with my cup, I focused on my shitty magic and sent a small spark of light to the fire. It crackled and sizzled, almost as if it wanted to sting me, but at least it worked. The fire restarted and as it spread to the wood, it grew bigger and hotter.

I leaned into it, glad for the warmth. I had been trying to forget it was so cold.

For the next thirty minutes, I sat beside Levi and the fire and tried working on my magic. I reached for it, tried to hold it, to command it, to mold it, but it was stubborn as hell. Several times, I grunted in frustration and thought about giving up.

But I wasn't a quitter, and I needed my magic.

Levi grunted and I stared at him. He opened his eyes for two seconds, then closed them again, and groaned. He reached for his middle and touched over the now closed wound.

"What did you do?" His voice was rough, parched, and still he sounded angry.

"What did *you* do?" I gestured toward the mountain lions. "Decided to join a brawl?"

With a jerk, Levi sat up and stared at the mountain lions. "Nothing else came?"

"No," I said. He relaxed but groaned as he lay down again, his eyes closed. "You didn't go far. When you saw the animals were getting too close to me, you intervened." I paused. "And when you saw I was cold, you warmed me."

He didn't say anything, he didn't open his eyes, he barely moved. That was answer enough and it sent a jolt of hope through my chest. He cared, which meant the feeling was there. I had to find it and make him acknowledge it. Then perhaps he would remember.

I scooted closer to him. "Levi."

He groaned again—what was it with him and groaning and grunting?—and he turned around, giving me his back.

I gaped at his back, my mouth open. The prick!

"Levi!" I called, this time louder and harsher. "You can't ignore me, not while there's only the two of us here. You might not want to talk about—"

He spun around so fast and leaned over me, his lips peeled and his fangs showing. "You're getting on my nerves."

I stood my ground. "Good! Then maybe you'll pay attention to me."

"Pay attention to you?" he barked, his voice deep. "All I do is think about you! I can't get you out of my head, no matter what I do!"

My heart squeezed. He had said something similar to me not long ago. I reached up and laid my hand on his hard chest. "It's because we're connected, you and I."

He snarled. "We have nothin—"

His head jerked to the side and his eyes scanned the line of trees. I was about to yell at him when I heard it too.

The snap of a twig and the ruffle of leaves.

Slowly, Levi stood and unfurled his huge wings behind him. He snarled at the trees.

A moment later, five figures walked past the trees and into our direct line of sight.

I gasped.

The men I had almost run into when exiting the bakery.

"What?" I muttered.

Gold-Tooth smiled at me, though it was a nervous one. "Surprised to see us, doll? We recognized you. You're the angel everyone is after."

The scarred one frowned at Levi. "Though, we thought you were alone."

Levi snarled at them. "Two lion shifters, and three half-demons. This should be easy."

In a flash, he pushed from the ground, flap his wings once, and landed on top of Gold-Tooth. The others jumped on Levi, except for the scarred one, who dodged Levi's wing-span and came directly for me.

I called my sword. It appeared in my hand and I swung it wide. He jumped back, snarling. His arms shifted into lion claws and his teeth elongated into fangs. He came at me again with his claws and teeth, but I parried his attack.

A darkfire bolt zipped past my head.

One of the half-demons who had snuck around Levi threw it, and I almost didn't dodge it in time. In doing so, I lost my balance and stumbled back.

The lion shifter lunged at me.

But he stopped midair, his eyes wide.

His body fell at my feet and behind him I could see Levi, the shifter's heart in his blood-soaked hand.

I did a quick glance around and saw all of them were

dead—and not just killed but butchered, with blood and body parts everywhere.

Puffing and grunting, Levi dropped the heart and came at me.

With murderous eyes, he grabbed my neck, drove me to the ground, pushing the air out of my lungs and snapped his fangs an inch from my face.

"Levi," I croaked. "It's me."

He snarled and pressed my throat tighter.

I croaked, but managed to touch him, to place my hand against his chest.

It was like a bucket of freezing water.

Levi sprung back several feet, his eyes wide as he stared at me, then took in the scene around us. Only now, he recognized me. Only now, he saw what he had done.

With a flap of his wings, Levi jumped up and away, zooming across the sky. And I was left alone amid this bloody mess.

16

I COULDN'T STAY THERE, BUT I DIDN'T WANT TO GO FAR IN CASE Levi came around again.

I walked to the nearest bank of the Red River and washed the blood from my neck and shirt and shaking hands.

What the hell had happened? It was like Levi had snapped and the demon had taken over, even if only for minutes.

But in those minutes, he had killed our enemies.

And he had advanced at me as if I was one of them.

He had almost butchered me too.

I didn't know what to think.

I sat on a rock a few feet from the water, and tried to think what to do. Should I wait for Levi? Before, he had stuck around and had come to help me when I needed him. What if this time he wasn't around? What if he had really left?

How long should I wait for him?

And what if I waited for him only to have him attack me?

I shivered.

I took to the skies and went to the same town as before. I

stopped at the gas station, where I charmed the young guy behind the counter to lend me his phone for a couple of minutes.

He was more than happy to oblige.

Thank goodness angels had good memories and I had learned most of my friends' numbers without much effort.

I started dialing Thea and stopped. Drake had left the underworld in a rush, to stop that crazy Sarki witch, and he was probably busy now trying to save Aurora from her, and Thea would be right there along with them.

Instead, I called Tanner's number.

"This better be good," he answered, his tone flat.

"Tanner, it's me, Ariella."

"Oh, it is good. Where the hell are you?"

I told him—I had to ask the clerk the name of the town—and Tanner guaranteed I would have a warlock to open a portal for me in no time. Apparently, the others were still locked in the underworld and were having trouble coming back.

It hadn't been my fault that I had left them all behind, but I was still sorry.

I waited by the gas station as instructed. Not ten minutes later, Boise walked out from the line of trees behind the pumps. He was friends with Aspen, and also worked directly with Keeran, the Warlock Lord.

"I'm here to take you to the underworld," he said, all formal.

I nodded and followed him back into the forest. Without a word, he opened the portal and I stepped through. I thought I would arrive in Tanner's throne room, but instead I was back at the underworld's gate. Of course, normal portals didn't work on the other side.

Lily was waiting for me. I thanked Boise for coming to pick me up and followed her into the underworld.

"How mad is he?" I asked.

"I have never seen King Tanner like this and I've known him for many years now," Lily told me.

Shit.

As expected, Tanner and Jasmin were waiting for me in the throne room. Lily stopped by the doorway and gestured for me to go alone. Awesome. Inhaling deeply, I walked toward the thrones.

Tanner became tenser the closer I got to them.

When I was finally about ten feet from them, he shot up from his throne. "What the hell happened out there?"

I let out a long sigh. I was sure Jasmin had already told him about the demon we encountered and Sarki, the witch who cursed Drake's daughter, but he didn't know the rest other than getting reports of Levi's escape.

"First, tell me, were you able to stop Ylena? And Sarki?"

"I asked you first—"

Jasmin rose from her throne and exchanged a heated glance with her brother, making him grunt and fall silent. "Unfortunately, no. There's something else you should know before you tell us what happened."

Oh, this couldn't be good. "What is it?"

"Time passes differently down in the mist," she said. "It goes by faster. When I came back here after helping Drake out, it had been only a handful of hours since we had left."

"Wait." I made some rash and surely inaccurate calculations in my heads. "But we were down there for days. That means ... Levi and Ylena were there for months."

She nodded. "We got a glimpse of Ylena when she escaped and she didn't look like an angel. How's Levi?"

I opened my mouth. Shut it again. That was why they had been so ragged, crazy, and dark. Because they had spent months lost in the mist.

I shook my head and told them what happened after Jasmin left with Drake.

With a sigh, I looked at Tanner. "I don't know what happened. I just know that I'm sorry for all of it."

Tanner pointed a finger at me. "You—"

Jasmin shot him a hard look and he immediately shut up. Staring at her, he inhaled deeply and let the air out slowly.

"Better?" Jasmin asked in a soft voice.

"Not really," he muttered, but at least he was composed and not yelling when he turned to me again. "I'm glad you were able to find Levi, but now we've got a big problem on our hands. Drake has been gone for only a couple of hours but he already called for a lockdown of DuMoir Castle, the Silverblood Estate, and the Silver Moon Academy."

"We offered him our help, but with Ylena on the loose, we need to divide our forces," Jasmin continued. "But first, we need to retrieve Rage and your friends."

Tanner nodded. "Demon hunters are waiting in front of the castle to go with you. Help them off the cliff, bring them here, and we'll reassemble when everyone is rested and clear minded."

"Yes," I said, feeling like a fledgling on her first day of guardian school.

"I'm coming with you." Jasmin descended the dais. "Are you ready to go, or do you need to—?"

"I'm ready to go," I said. I was tired, in need of a shower, but if I had been outside the mist for over a day, my friends were probably in there for who knew how long. We could all rest and clean up later.

A handful of demon hunters I hadn't met before waited for us at the castle's entrance. It was all the same. We walked a good distance, and then the shadow horses appeared.

When we were about an hour from the cliff's edge, a demon hunter shouted. "Stop!"

The horses slowed down to a halt.

"What happened?" Jasmin asked.

"There." The hunter pointed to the horizon.

Slowly, shadows formed in the distance ... no, not shadows. Silhouettes. People.

"By the light," I muttered, kicking the sides of my horse.

The animal jumped into a gallop and only slowed down when we came face to face with my friends—who were all also mounted on shadow horses.

My heart squeezed upon seeing Rage among them. "You're alive."

"Thanks to Zad and Lacey," he said. He did look like he had been beaten pretty badly, but I was certain he had died.

"Well done with the key," Wyatt said.

I had kicked the key down the cliff. "I was worried you wouldn't see it."

"It was pure luck," Farrah said.

"Where's Levi?" Lacey asked, concern clear on her face. "What happened?"

I let out a sigh. "Come on. I'll tell you everything on the way back to the castle."

17

I DIDN'T SLEEP WELL.

The shower was amazing, the bed was comfortable, and yet, every time I closed my eyes, I saw Levi with his bloody hand around my throat ready to kill me just like he did with those demons.

Restless, I woke up and was fortunate enough to find Lily outside the dining room.

"What can I do for you, Miss Ariella?"

"Is there anywhere I can exercise here? Run, more specifically."

"Of course." She guided me through a long hallway, down to a more intimate area of the castle, and showed me a large door that opened up to a giant gym with lots of equipment. "I believe you can run in here."

I looked around. There was no track, but there were four treadmills. Why four, though? Did anyone else besides Tanner and Jasmin use this room?

I shook my head. That didn't matter to me at all. "Thank you," I said to the demon as I walked into the gym.

I hopped on one of the treadmills and turned it on. I started slow, with a brisk walk, but it didn't take long for me to speed it up and run.

While running, I blanked out my mind. I focused only on my breathing, the beating of my heart, and my steps. Every time my mind wandered, I forced it to focus.

It worked. For forty minutes, I ran without really stressing or worrying about anything.

It was a pleasant change.

Shame it didn't last.

I went back to my bedroom, took a nice, hot shower, put on some jean leggings, a tank top, my now magically cleaned leather jacket, and boots, and headed back to the dining room.

And this time, almost everyone was already there for breakfast—Farrah, Wyatt, Zad, Lacey, and Rage.

"You look better," I told Rage, as I took a place between Farrah and Lacey.

He nodded. "Thanks to Lacey. She healed me a little more last night."

She smiled at him. "You're welcome."

I glanced from Lacey to Rage, back to Lacey. Was I sensing something here, or was it just me?

"How did you sleep?" Farrah asked me.

I shook my head. "Not very well."

"Me neither," she said.

"I don't think any of us did," Wyatt said.

"Ain't that the truth?" Tanner's voice rang through the room as he and Jasmin walked in.

"Calm down, Tanner," Jasmin muttered. "We talked about this." She took one of the heads of the long table while Tanner took the other. "Lily, we're ready."

Lily appeared from a side door with two lesser demons who brought out heaps of food and deposited it in the middle of the table. There were pancakes, waffles, all kinds of eggs, bacon, toast, muffins, bagels, croissants, fruits, juices, three kinds of coffee, and even hot chocolate. The delicious scent of it all tickled my nose and my mouth watered.

For a few minutes, the only sound on the room was of everyone piling up their plates and eating.

Tanner ate only a little and didn't waste time.

"With Lord Drake not calling the shots at the moment, we need to come up with a plan ourselves," he said, his voice unusually serious. This pissed off Tanner was rubbing me the wrong way. "Anyone have any ideas?"

"So, just to recap," Farrah started. "We need to capture Ylena and Levi, return Levi to his old self, stop Rhodes, and save Elysium?"

"You say that as if it was an easy to-do list," Rage mused.

"Definitely not easy, but we need to know all the details before we come up with a plan, no?" she said.

Frowning, Rage nodded.

"I think the first thing is to figure out where Ylena and Levi would have gone," Lacey said. She looked at me for a second. "I think Levi would be going after Ylena."

"And we heard Rhodes is after Ylena too," Jasmin said.

I frowned. "How?" And more importantly, "Why?"

"We might not have a handle on the entire underworld yet, but we do have plenty of connections in the human realm," Tanner said. "As for why ... to kill her? To shut her up? To bring her back to their side since she's strong? Who knows?"

"And who cares?" Rage said. "The important thing is stopping both of them."

"So what?" Zad asked. "We go after Rhodes and Ylena?"

"And Levi," Lacey said. "He'll be where they are."

"And I think I know where Ylena will be," I said. "Well, that's not true. She doesn't know *where*, but I do know what she's after."

"The Scarlet Hex Dagger," Zad said.

I nodded.

"So, one more item for that list," Jasmin said. "To find the dagger before Ylena and put it in a secure place, where no one, not even us, can access it."

"Do we even know what the dagger does?" Tanner asked. "What if it's a simple dagger and everyone is going crazy over it?"

"It can't be a simple dagger," Lacey said.

I nodded. "Molraz went to great lengths to secure it, and then look at everything Ylena and Rhodes did to get their hands on it. Whatever this dagger does, it can't be good."

"I agree that when we find it, we should secure it," Farrah said. "No matter what it does. Better safe than sorry."

Jasmin and Tanner exchanged a long, tense look.

The king of the underworld exhaled. "Agreed."

"So, where's the dagger?" Wyatt asked me.

Shit.

I opened my mouth but closed it when Lily appeared in the main doorway. "You have a visitor," she said, looking from Tanner, to Jasmin, to me.

She stepped aside and gestured to Abbie.

I turned on my seat to face her. "Abbie, everything okay?"

She nodded. "I think so." She glanced at King Tanner. "May I?"

"Of course." He gestured for her to walk in. "You're a guest."

"Thank you." She walked toward me and held a book up, which I only noticed now.

I stood. "What's that?"

"My great-grandmother's diary." She turned the book. It was small, with a torn leather cover, and yellowed pages. "She wrote about the dagger."

"What?"

She opened the book and handed it to me. I held the book and stared at the neat handwriting on the pages. On half of one page, there was a drawing of the dagger.

Now everyone was up from their seats and hovering around us.

Abbie pointed to a paragraph on the page. "She says the dagger can change a supernatural being, including their powers."

"How?" Tanner asked. He was right beside us, his eyes on the book.

"My great-grandmother never tested it, but she knew this. I don't know how, it doesn't say. At least not the parts I've read." Abbie glanced at me. "According to her, the one yielding the dagger has to have immense power, otherwise they will be changed too."

"But how does it work?" Jasmin asked. She was right beside Tanner.

"Again, this is only theory," Abbie warned, "but she says the dagger bearer should hold the dagger to the supernatural's chest, push its power inside him, and order it to change him, and apparently, the dagger will know what exactly you want to change."

I scanned the page. "Does she mention how it changes them?"

Abbie nodded. "You can make them mortal, weak, power-less, or if they are good, you can make them evil."

I sucked in a sharp.

"What if they are evil and you want to turn them good?" Lacey asked exactly what I was thinking.

Abbie showed her a small smile. "That too."

Lacey looked at me and I held her gaze, then I turned to Tanner and Jasmin. "I might be jumping to conclusions here, but what if Ylena and Rhodes wanted the dagger to make Adona mortal? She would be killable."

"And they would become the rulers," Tanner mused, his voice low.

"That seems plausible," Jasmin said, a crease between her delicate brows.

"Let's say that's not their plan," Zad said. "This is still a powerful dagger. We can't let them get it."

Tanner stared at me. "We need to secure the dagger."

I had run from that thing for so long, it had brought so much pain to me and to Elysium, I wasn't eager to get it again.

But I knew he was right.

We had to get the dagger before someone else happened upon it.

I stared at the king of the underworld. "I have one condition."

His brows furrowed. "And what is that?"

"Before we secure the dagger, we use it ... on Levi."

18

I KNEW LACEY HAD HAD THE SAME IDEA AS ME. USE THE Scarlet Hex Dagger to expel the darkness from Levi and bring him back to his old self.

Of course, Tanner, Zad, and Rage voiced their distaste. But it wasn't a negotiation, not really.

I knew this step complicated things, but it would be the easiest way to have Levi back. And once we had him back, he would be a great force on our side, fighting alongside us.

So, after breakfast Tanner told us to get ready. "We'll assemble a small team and leave at noon." He turned to Lily. "I'll need a glass of whiskey."

She nodded and left to procure it.

Jasmin glared at him. "It's eight in the morning."

"In the human world," he retorted. "Here, it is whatever the hell we want it to be."

I frowned at Tanner. Was he always like this underneath the fun, bickering guy I had met before? Or had circumstances become so grim, it erased his fun side?

Tanner took his seat while he waited for Lily. With a

groan, Jasmin took the chair to his right. "Maybe I should have a glass too."

As everyone filed out of the dining room—Abbie followed Lacey out—I approached them. I stopped behind one of the tall chairs and looked at the siblings. "I know Lord Drake is preoccupied, but maybe we should keep him and DuMoir Castle informed of what's going on."

Tanner nodded. "I'll call him."

"Thank you," I said.

"Calling Drake doesn't require thanks."

"Not just that, but for agreeing to save Levi, and organizing a team to help me."

"That dagger is too powerful, and it seems we're all doomed if we don't help, so ..." He waved his arm wide. "I'm doing what any decent leader would do."

Jasmin rolled her eyes. "He wants compliments, Ariella. Right now, we should say he's doing a fabulous job with the underworld, and there's no better king than him."

"A lie and we all know it," he said, a coldness in his tone I had never heard before.

"Yes, but we've talked about this before," Jasmin said. "Fake it until you make it. No one is born knowing how to rule. You'll learn, and the best way to learn it is on the job."

"It's a messy way to learn."

"Besides, you're not alone. You have me, and Erin and all of the demon hunters, and Lord Drake and DuMoir Castle. Anything you need, you know they will help."

"But that makes us look weak, unprepared. What if someone realizes we're in way over our heads and decides to attack us head on? I don't really mind not being king, but I do mind if a person worse than me takes over."

Jasmin placed her hand on Tanner's arm. "And that's why you're the best for this job."

I stared at the siblings. They'd always been chatty, snobby, and crazy and uncaring. They bickered all the time, and I thought that was their normal day.

Unless that was a shield, a facade so the world thought they were powerful.

Maybe I was overthinking things, but seeing them like this, with their walls down, showing their worries, and being there for each other, was heartwarming.

"I agree with Jasmin," I said. Both of them looked at me as if surprised I was still there. "The fact that you feel you're unworthy, and you want to protect this realm makes you a good candidate to be king."

Tanner frowned. "Wait, I never said unworthy."

I smiled. Jasmin laughed. "Ah, that's awesome. Please continue. Maybe he'll bicker with someone else other than me."

Lily came back with a glass of whiskey and another of wine.

"I should go get ready," I said.

I left the siblings alone in the dining room. As I turned the first corner, I bumped into Lacey and Abbie.

"There you are," Lacey said.

Abbie held the diary. After the revelations, I had returned it to her, though I was dying to read it. "Are you ready?"

I shook my head. "But I'll never be, so we should get this over with." She nodded. "Are you coming with us? We might need your help with Levi."

"That isn't a bad idea," Lacey said. "You said we'll need someone with immense power to wield the dagger. That will be you, for sure."

She chewed the inside of her cheek. "I should warn Maggie, then. I told her I would be back soon."

"Of course," I said, relieved she was coming. "Meet us at the gate at noon?"

"For sure. But for now ..." She handed me the journal. "I know you're probably curious about the dagger, so why don't you read until it's time to leave. Unless you have too much to do until—"

I took the diary. "No, if everything works out, we won't be gone long." I glanced at my phone. I had two hours to read. "Thank you."

"My pleasure." She waved at us and left, as if she knew exactly how to navigate the castle.

Maybe she did.

"How about you?" I asked Lacey. "Need to get ready?"

"I'm just going to stop by my room to get supplies, maybe the castle's apothecary, but then I'll be free."

"Come find me when you're done," I said. "It would be good to read this with you. I know you're interested too."

"I will." She stared at the book in my arms. "Hopefully, we'll find something useful in these pages."

"Hopefully." I hugged the book tighter. "And then we'll save your brother."

THE BOOK DIDN'T HAVE MUCH MORE than what Abbie had already told us.

If the person wielding the dagger wasn't strong enough, she would change or become magicless.

I had already lost my magic once, and as much as it wasn't the same as before, I wasn't willing to lose it again.

Besides, I wasn't powerful enough. It had to be someone else.

At noon, we met at the castle's entrance: me, Lacey, Farrah, Wyatt, Zad, Tanner, Jasmin, and Rage.

We walked together to the gate, where Tanner and Jasmin were left behind.

"Good luck," the king of the underworld said.

"It'll all work out," Jasmin added.

At first, both of them talked about coming with us, but after some discussion, we all agreed that exposing the rulers of the underworld to the angels wasn't a good idea. Tanner seemed to hate that he had to stay, but he knew what was at stake. He needed to stay alive to protect the underworld.

We met Abbie outside the gates.

"I was certain Maggie would have come this time," Lacey said.

"She tried, but as the next in line to take over the hall if something happens to me, I forbade her," Abbie explained.

"Nothing will happen to you," I said. Lacey nodded in agreement.

The demon hunters Ava, Harvey, Doreen, and Andre joined us. I had met all of them before, and knew Ava and Harvey had been engaged for about two years now.

"Erin and Rey apologize for not being here," Ava said, sounding bored. "They had other stuff to do."

"The stuff is actually a call from Archangel Rhodes," Harvey explained.

"A call?" That piqued my interest.

"Yeah, he sent a couple of messages to reschedule the meeting," Doreen said, "but Erin and Rey keep inventing excuses. He then asked for a call." I couldn't help but stare at her beautiful auburn hair.

"If Rhodes insists, they will set a meeting date for two months out," Andre said. He was a handsome black man, built like a wall and with long dreadlocks.

"By then we should have all of this solved," Zad said. "Hopefully."

"Hopefully," I muttered in agreement.

Aspen arrived soon after.

"Thank you for coming," Rage told him.

"Part of my work," he said, though he didn't sound excited. I had seen Aspen do this before, where he created portals for us. That had to get old fast.

Aspen opened a portal and gestured for us to get through. I went in first, and I took in the view. We were atop a hill over-looking the Colorado River. My friends, along with Aspen, stepped through the portal. He had agreed to stay with us since we would need him when it was time to come back, and we didn't know when that would be.

The plan was for us to get the dagger, lure Levi, turn him, and go back to the underworld.

"This place is beautiful," Lacey said, taking in the view.

I nodded. "I washed out after jumping from the cliff somewhere along this bank." I pointed to the river. "Two Mojave kids found me and called their elders."

I hadn't revealed all the details of where exactly the dagger was. I had told them to come along with me. And they did.

It filled my heart that they trusted me this much.

"You were taken in by the Mojave people?" Farrah asked.

"Not exactly." I jerked my chin to the opposite side of the river, toward the desert and the mountains in the distance. Joshua trees were the only green thing around. "Come on. It's not far from here."

We walked inland for about fifteen minutes and saw absolutely nothing but the bleak, but beautiful landscape. Everyone was quiet, but I could sense their restlessness in the air. They wanted to know exactly where we were going.

"Please, tell me you didn't stash the dagger under a rock," Ava said. She was joking, but there was a little uncertainty to her statement.

"Well, the thought did pass my mind when I was being dragged away from the river." I chuckled. "But no."

The landscape changed slightly. The Joshua trees became bigger and closer together. Trusting my memory, I continued through the trees to where the terrain fell abruptly. About sixty feet down was what looked like an enchanted valley: green grass and colorful flowers surrounded a small wooden cottage, with a smoking chimney. All of it sheltered by a thick line of full green trees.

"We're here," I whispered.

A woman with long, black hair tied in a loose braid walked out of the cottage, a washcloth in her hands.

She looked up, directly at me. "I've been expecting you."

19

MY FRIENDS STARED AT THE WOMAN.

"Come on," I said, showing them the hidden path along the hill. They followed me silently.

The woman waited for us at the bottom of the stairs.

"Sorry it took me so long," I said.

"Nonsense." She waved me off. "I'm glad you're okay." She opened her arms and embraced me. "How have you been?"

"Not so great," I said, hugging her back. In a way, being here, seeing her again, it brought so many emotions, so many memories I had tried to forget. I pulled back, cleared my throat, and turned to my friends. "Guys, this is Topaz."

"Hello there," Topaz said with a small smile, showing off how her bright white teeth contrasted with her smooth, light brown skin.

Wyatt sniffed the air. "You're a witch."

Topaz nodded. "You're right, young man."

Though she looked like was she was forty, Topaz was actually over eighty years old. That happened to most witches, and from the little I knew, she was a powerful one.

And for some reason she never disclosed to me, she had been living quietly in the Fort Mojave Reservation for at least a decade.

Lacey pushed through our friends until she was standing just two feet from Topaz. "I know you."

Topaz's face paled. "Lacey," she whispered.

I stared from one to the other. "Wait. What's going on?"

"Topaz is from my coven," Lacey said, her wide eyes fixed on the witch.

And the way she said Topaz wasn't lost on me. I kind of figured that a person in hiding would change her name. I mean, even I had changed my name for a while.

"And what coven is that?" Ava asked. She knew that so far Lacey hadn't revealed anything about her coven to me or the others. Only Levi knew to which coven she belonged.

"I thought you were dead," Lacey said, her tone flat. Slowly her eyes went from wide to narrowed, and her surprised features changed to ... was that anger?

"I—" Topaz started.

"Never mind," Lacey snapped, cutting the older woman off. "We're here for a reason." She nodded to me, telling me to go on.

With what?

Did she want me to ignore her animosity? I looked from Lacey to Topaz, the wildest ideas crossing my mind. I remembered Levi telling me Lacey's mother had died when she was young, and now Lacey said she thought Topaz was dead and she clearly wasn't.

But that was ridiculous. Right?

Well, after finding out Ylena was Levi's mother, I didn't doubt anything anymore.

However, right at this moment, Lacey didn't seem to want

to dwell on it. She crossed her arms, huffed, and jerked her chin at me, as if telling me to hurry up.

Okay then.

I cleared my throat. Pretending nothing happened, I introduced the others to Topaz, telling her their names, kinds, and if there was one, their jobs. The witch had an incredible memory, and in my brief time here, I had play-tested her many times.

"The Mojave kids brought me to her and she nursed me back to life," I told my friends.

Rage frowned. "The kids brought Ariella to you. So, the Mojave people know you're here?"

"Yes, we have an agreement." She folded the towel in her hands, almost wrangling it with brisk movements. "I believe I know why you're here."

I nodded. "Sorry I didn't come alone. It was safer this way."

"I know." She glanced at all my friends, except for Lacey. "Follow me."

She turned her back to us and walked toward the rocky wall. She stopped in front of a random spot, waved her hand, and the rock shimmered until it disappeared, giving away to a five-by-eight foot entrance.

She extended her hand, palm up, and a ball of light poofed into existence. She pushed the ball forward and it floated in the air past the entrance. She gestured for me to go in first.

Holding my breath, I stepped through.

The hidden entrance gave way to a small cave, with nothing remarkable on the inside. At first glance, a person would wonder why Topaz had hidden this place.

I knew better.

I walked to the back of the space, knelt beside the wall, grabbed a large stone that fit perfectly in the ground, and pushed it aside.

Under the stone was a dark hole, the size of a large drawer, or a medium suitcase. And inside were a few items, all wrapped with enchanted cloth. According to Topaz, if I tried taking any of the other items hidden in that hole that didn't belong to me, I would get shocked, and if I tried again, the shock could debilitate me. If I kept going, it would kill me.

So, I never tested that theory.

I reached inside and picked up the item that was a couple of inches wide and as long as my forearm, enveloped in a navy cloth.

I shuddered, thinking of how powerful this dagger was. Much more than I first thought when I took it.

Holding it in my hand, I stood up. All of my friends were inside the cave now, along with Topaz, the yellowish light floating near the ceiling casting dark shadows under their faces.

"Is that it?" Lacey asked, her voice thin.

Slowly, I laid the dagger in one of my palms, unwrapped the cloth, and I sucked in a sharp breath. There it was. The Scarlet Hex Dagger.

I had forgotten how simple but beautiful it was with its short silver hilt, a red gem on the pommel, and the shiny blade that, when twisted to one side or the other, showed a faint red tint.

"It is," I said, not believing it. Here it was. The dagger was in my hands again.

And this was dangerous. We needed to do what we came to do and hide it again.

I turned to Topaz. "We need your help with one more thing."

TOPAZ HAD WORKED HARD to secure an agreement with the Mojave tribe so she could occupy this corner of their land. And yet, I had shown up at her doorstep five years ago, beaten and bloody, within an inch of my life.

And now I was here again, asking another favor.

She wasn't happy about it, especially because we would have to go to an open field for the next step. But she didn't complain. Not out loud, at least.

She marched ahead of us, taking the lead and guiding us farther into the Mojave land, away from their settlements—and her place—where we could do the spell without attracting unwanted attention.

We walked under the harsh sun for over thirty minutes, until we were standing in a large clearing among tall Joshua trees.

Zad and the demon hunters spread out through the clearing, as if patrolling the area to keep our enemies out.

Hopefully, no one knew where we were and no enemy would show up.

Well, except for Levi.

And maybe Ylena.

Abbie pulled out chalk from her dress's pocket. "I'll draw the circle."

"Do you have more chalk?" Lacey asked.

Abbie handed her a second piece of chalk and the two of them set out to draw a large witch's circle in the center of the clearing. Aspen stood back, waiting for the circle to be ready.

And Farrah knew me too well. She took Wyatt's hand and went to help the others.

As for me ... I couldn't help any longer.

I turned to Topaz and whispered, "You're from Lacey's coven? And she thought you were dead? Care to explain?"

Topaz regarded me with her kind brown eyes. "What do you know about my life?"

She hadn't revealed much in the couple of weeks I had stayed with her. "Almost nothing."

"Exactly. Why do you think it'll change now?"

I rolled my eyes at her. "Fine. Don't answer. Lacey will tell me."

"I don't think she will."

I gaped at her. "Is it that bad?"

"I'm not sure."

"What does that even mean?" I frowned. "Are you her mother?"

Topaz stared at me, a glint I couldn't place in her eyes. "No."

That word echoed in my ears, hard and absolute. All right. I believed that, but then ... "What are you? To her, I mean?"

The witch shook her head. "Drop it, Ariella."

"You know I won't—"

"It's done," Abbie announced, unaware she was disrupting my interrogation.

Ignoring me, Topaz looked at the warlock. "Are you ready?"

Aspen stepped forward, to the edge of the circle. "I'm ready."

"Witches and warlock, position." Topaz approached the

circle. Lacey, Abbie, and Aspen spread out, standing on equidistant four points around the circle.

The others stayed back.

I handed the dagger to Topaz. We had agreed she was probably the most powerful of us, but Lacey, Abbie, and Aspen would send their magic to enhance Topaz's, just in case.

I would stay on the sidelines, watching and praying it worked.

Topaz picked up the dagger and nodded at Aspen.

He put one step inside the circle, closed his eyes, and raised his hands. I felt the tug of his magic reaching inside of me. To open the portal where Levi was without knowing, Aspen would use the bond. He said that theoretically, the bond connected us all the time, even if sometimes it felt muted.

A purple ball appeared over Aspen's hand, and it grew and grew. "Almost there," he said, and I had an idea that he was holding the bond's line and searching.

The ball flattened and became a large portal.

With an outstretched hand, Aspen tugged hard on an invisible line.

Levi burst from the portal, roaring like a mad animal. His red eyes zeroed in on Aspen. He swiped his big claws, but thankfully, Aspen stepped back and out of the circle, missing the strike by an inch.

Just as the portal was closing, someone else flew through it.

Ylena.

She went directly for Levi, who turned to continue their battle.

But we knew that was a possibility and we were ready.

Lacey and Abbie threw their magic out, tying Ylena and pulling her back, until she stood in a small witch circle, inside the bigger one.

Still blinded by her rage, Ylena flapped her dark wings and made for Levi but she hit the circle's invisible wall and fell back, her wings folding awkwardly underneath her.

Levi had also charged Ylena and met the wall's barrier. Fangs bared, he turned around, finally stopping to see what was going on. He snarled at Abbie, glanced over at Lacey as if he didn't know her, snapped his teeth at Aspen, and froze when he saw the dagger in Topaz's hands.

"Levi," I said.

He shifted his gaze to me. "You again."

"Yes, me." I lifted my chin. "I waited for you, you know? I thought you would come back, like you did before. But hours passed and nothing." He stared at me, anger and frustration flashing in his eyes. "Did you ignore the bond? Or did you feel it?" I held a finger up. "Don't answer that." I glanced at Ylena. "I see you quickly found her."

"It wasn't that quick," he said, his voice still like a monster's.

"And yet, you found her."

Ylena smiled at me, looking more like a depraved demon than an archangel. "You say you two are connected. He and I are connected too."

I frowned. "Oh, I know. But do you? Do you know why you're connected? How?"

The two of them seemed lost with my question.

"Got it!" Topaz yelled.

I took a step back as she pointed the dagger at Levi. A line of red light stretched from the tip of the blade to Levi's chest, and before he could register what was happening, the line pushed inside of him, and he fell to his knees, roaring.

"The dagger!" Ylena screamed and rammed into the invisible wall again.

Aspen lifted his hand and the wall around the smaller circle became a light gray, like frosted glass. The angel punched the wall and screamed, but the sound was muffled.

And we could focus.

Topaz gritted her teeth. "Turn this demon back to what he was," she said, ordering the dagger. "Change him back to the man he was."

A spark of magic traveled through the red line, and Levi yelled when it entered him.

His arms were as spread out as his big wings, with his neck stretched, his head tilted up.

"Don't resist it," I told him, but I wasn't sure he was listening.

Lacey, Abbie, and Aspen lifted their arms to their sides, and their magic traveled like a wave around them all, connecting the four of them, and feeding into Topaz.

"Turn this demon back to what he was!" Topaz yelled. The spark traveled from the blade to Levi's chest again, and he half yelled, half snarled.

My heart tugged. He was in pain, and I was responsible for this.

But it had to be done. That was the only way he would be himself again.

With a grunt, Topaz sank to her knees.

I knelt beside her, the others moved but Lacey shouted, "No one move! Send more of your magic to Topaz. To the blade!"

The line connected them became brighter, thicker, and

the magic flowed into Topaz, through the blade, and into Levi.

He gritted his teeth.

"He's resisting it," Topaz said, her words barely a whisper. "I can't hold this up for long."

"You have to. It is the only way."

She shook her head. "He's fighting *me*."

"What?"

Her brown eyes fixed into mine. "Trust me." Topaz pushed the dagger into my hands. I tried pulling away, but she held on to me. "Trust me," she whispered again.

And so I did.

She transferred the dagger to me, and without breaking contact, moved her hands to lay on top of mine. A jolt rushed through me as the magic now passed from Topaz, to me, to the dagger, into Levi.

"Now, it's your turn," she said. "Say your intentions. Mix them with the magic."

I looked at Levi. "Come back to me," I said, low, timid.

No, this wouldn't do. Hoisting Topaz with me, I stood, tall and proud, and opened up myself, my magic, my feelings. I let them mingle with the others' magic, I let it envelop everything, sugarcoating the intent with my need to have him back.

I inhaled deeply and let it all out. "Come back to me, Levi. This is not who you are. You pretend to be this big, bad demon, like the one you are now, but that's not really you." My chest tightened. "You're loyal, you're caring, and you're honest." Tears burned the back of my eyes. "You're someone I had no intention of meeting, let alone get attached to, but now I can't imagine my life without you in it." A lump formed in my throat. "And I know you feel the same, so come back to me!"

I pushed the magic with all my might. The line was thicker than my arm and it tremble with a spark that exploded in Levi's chest.

Levi fell back, the line disappeared, and the flow of magic ceased.

I stared at him, at the dagger, at Topaz. "What happened? Is it done?"

Her wide eyes were as clueless as mine.

I passed the dagger back to her and rushed to Levi. I knelt beside him two seconds before Lacey did.

A shudder coursed through Levi's body and it changed.

Gone was his gray skin, the dark veins. His horns and wings retreated, his hair shortened, and the torn pants he had on seemed a little loose now.

He shuddered again, and then exhaled slowly as he opened his eyes.

And stared right at me.

"I'm here, sweetheart."

20

I THREW MYSELF OVER HIM, MY ARMS WRAPPING AROUND HIS neck, and half of my torso over his. He grunted but wound one arm around my waist and held me tight.

"By the light, I haven't felt this relieved in a while," I said.

Levi buried his face in my neck, placed a gentle kiss under my ear, and whispered, "I missed you, sweetheart."

Lacey cleared her throat. "We don't want to see anything not PG rated."

Reluctantly, Levi and I pulled apart, but I kept my hand on his arm as we stood. Once on our feet, he slid my hand down and entwined his fingers with mine.

"Thank you," Levi said, first staring at me, then his sister, and then at everyone else. I knew these words weren't easy for him to say, and I was sure he wouldn't repeat them for a while, but I could see the emotion in his blue eyes.

"That explosion released a lot of magic, and it felt like a beacon." Topaz approached us and handed me the dagger. "You should go before trouble finds you."

"Trouble always finds me." I took the dagger from her.

Levi's eyes narrowed as he stared at the dagger.

"What about her?" Abbie asked.

We all turned to the smaller circle, where the mad angel still yelled and punched the wall.

A growl started low in Levi's chest.

"You guys go," Topaz said, "and I'll keep her locked in here for the rest of the day."

"What if she attacks you?" Aspen said.

"She can try, but she won't be able to." Topaz offered us a small smile. "My cottage is warded and only those with no ill intentions can approach it."

"But she's powerful," I said.

"Are you doubting my powers?" Topaz feigned annoyance.

"Then let's go," Lacey said, her voice still flat.

I let go of Levi's hand and reached for Topaz. "Thank you for—"

My words died as a new sound reached my ears.

The zooming of something approaching fast.

Angels.

I looked up, and sure enough, a dozen or more angels dressed in their white and silver battle uniforms flew directly at us.

"I'm on it," Aspen said, as he moved his hands fast and started opening a portal.

A light bolt zipped from behind us, hitting Aspen's side, and stopping the spell. He fell backward, and for a moment I feared he was dead, but then Lacey knelt beside him and told us he was just injured.

Behind us, dozens of new angels approached, and these were much closer than the others.

"Shit," Levi muttered.

"Get ready!" Ava yelled.

The demon hunters formed a wide circle around us. Wyatt, Farrah, and Zad joined them.

Lacey put her hand over Aspen's wound, closed her eyes, and three seconds later, pulled her hand back. The wound was gone.

"Thank you," Aspen said.

"Can't you open a portal?" Zad asked Abbie.

She shook her head. "My portals are tethered to the Grand Eternity Hall. Only I can go there." She pressed her lips for a second. "And I won't open one to the hall now."

She was right. The angels were too close already, and they would be upon us in a minute or less. By the time she cast the portal and we all crossed, an angel or ten might cross with us.

We couldn't risk it.

Besides, I knew Abbie's instincts were to protect the hall. Bringing this many supernaturals there probably felt wrong.

Rage frowned at me. "You can't let them get the dagger."

I wrapped the cloth around it again and tucked it in the waist of my pants, a little sideways, so it wouldn't bother me during the fight.

Topaz touched the frosted wall of Ylena's circle. A jolt of electricity coursed through it. Inside, Ylena yelp as the electricity zapped her, and she fell to the ground. "She'll be out for a few minutes," the witch said.

I nodded, glad to have one less thing to worry about now.

"Everyone, protect Ariella," Rage said, loud and clear. "We can't let them get to her."

All of my friends surrounded me, forming a circle around Levi and me.

Levi grabbed my hand again and squeezed tight, his eyes on the sky as the angels got closer.

I recognized Julien and Izrail among the first dozen, and when I glanced at the bigger group, I saw none other than Archangel Rhodes leading them. And right by his side was Archangel Sariel. Behind them, I saw Mihael and Briela, an angel who had been two years behind me at the academy. I didn't recognize any of the others, but I did count again.

In total, there were twenty-eight angels, against fourteen of us.

And Ylena, who didn't count at the moment.

As expected, Rhodes stopped a safe way from us, but Sariel continued, leading the angels closer. When they were in range, the angels sped up while throwing light magic at us.

The witches and the warlock create a shield over us, to give us some time. But as we called our magic and held our weapons, the angels landed and surrounded us.

"Ariella," Sariel called me, sounding bored. "Tell your friends to surrender. If you bring the dagger to me, they won't be harmed."

"Why would I?" I asked, trying to feel as bold as my words. "You only have twice our number. I think we can take you."

"In a matter of minutes, a hundred angels will be upon you." A wicked smile spread over Sariel's pale lips. "There's no hope."

"There's always hope," Zad said.

Sariel glanced at him. "Fancy seeing you here, Zadkiel. Realize now why your dear mentor let you stay away?" She laughed, but it was short-lived. "You have five seconds to decide, Ariella. What is it going to be? Are you going to let your friends die because you're stubborn?"

I pressed my lips and glanced at my friends.

"Don't fall for it," Lacey whispered.

"Don't worry about us," Farrah said, equally low.

"Protect the dagger," Rage reminded me.

It pained me to know that if we didn't win in the next few minutes, we would all die, but it also filled me with pride to know my friends had my back.

Startling me, Rage lifted his spear. "We have minutes to kill them all!" he shouted.

The witches dropped the shield and Rage sent a big bolt of darkfire at Sariel.

And the battle started.

Levi let go of my hand as the flock of angels descended upon us. He quickly transformed into his demon self, grabbed the neck of an angel before he could land, and cracked his head on the ground.

I flinched with the violence but had my own problems to take care of as two angels advanced on me—Julien and Izrail. I called my sword and swung at them.

"Still don't have your magic?" Julien asked, his tone teasing. "What a shame." He cast a bolt of light magic and threw it at my face.

I twisted fast and dodged it, but not before I felt the heat of the bolt on my cheek.

When I twisted back, Julien was right at my side, his magic ready to hit me. But I was quicker. I leaned to the left to avoid the hit, and swung my sword wide, cutting his bicep.

He screamed and let go of his magic.

I lifted my sword, poised at his heart.

His eyes met mine.

I hesitated.

"So weak," Izrail said from my right. Before I could step away, he brought his sword up and hit the pommel on my temple.

For a second or two, my vision filled with black spots and my head rattled.

I blinked, forcing my mind to clear.

Lost, I stepped back.

And heard a growl.

Levi turned to Julien and Izrail. Without ceremony, he sent a snake of darkfire at Julien, wrapped around him tightly. The angel fell to the ground, squirming against the dark smoky ropes around him.

Then Levi bared his teeth at Izrail.

Izrail's face became paler. His arms trembled as he moved his hands and tried to summon his magic. But Levi was too fast for him. The demon lifted Izrail by his throat, placed his hand on the angel's chest, and discharged his magic like an electrical jolt.

Izrail shook, his eyes rolled back, and when Levi let him go, the angel fell in a heap on the ground, right beside Julien, who screamed again.

With a deadly gaze, Levi turned to me and for a moment, I was scared he had gone back to being the same as before. The demon who had been lost to the darkness.

But he blinked, and the darkness fell away.

"Are you okay?" he asked.

"I'm—"

A light whip cut the air between Levi and me, and we both turned to see Sariel and two other angels standing too close for comfort.

Sariel wrapped the whip around her forearm. "Last chance, Ariella."

I looked around—the battle raged, and though I could see some of them were hurt, my friends were holding on. I couldn't give up now.

"Go fuck yourself," I said.

Levi scoffed and Sariel's face turned red.

Someone moved behind Sariel.

Rhodes.

He was flying to where Ylena was imprisoned. A swell of rage and panic flooded my veins.

I tried sidestepping Sariel, but she moved with me. "Where do you think you're going?"

Levi sent a bolt of darkfire at Sariel's face. She barely had time to step back and avoid it. She stared at him with wide eyes.

"Go," he mouthed at me before engaging Sariel and keeping her occupied.

I ran to Rhodes as he reached for the barrier around the circle containing Ylena.

"Stop!" I shouted without really thinking.

The archangel glanced at me. "Or what?"

I halted and swallowed hard. "Whatever it is you want to do." My shoulders sag. "Just stop, Rhodes. All of it."

He let out a hollow laugh. "Dear Ariella, always so sweet and innocent. You have no idea how this world works, and never will."

He turned back to the circle and I reached for him, intent on stopping him.

But two sets of arms wrapped around mine from behind and kept me in place.

"No!" I jerked against the hold of two angels.

A bolt of red magic hit Rhodes in the shoulder. With a snarl, he spun around and faced Topaz. "Oh, the witch who cast this circle. Exactly who I need." His Celestial sword appeared in his hand, almost twice the size of mine. "This should be fun."

He came at her with his sword, but Topaz wasn't fooled. She raised a barrier with her magic and cast bolts from that barrier to Rhodes.

Fast like lightning, he cut through those bolts with his sword as if they were slow and made of paper. With each swing of his sword, he advanced, until he struck his sword on the barrier, breaking it.

The force of the impact rattled Topaz's powers and she stumbled back while casting another bolt. But Rhodes grabbed her wrist before she could throw it at him and pushed her hand into her chest.

Topaz's magic hit herself and she fell back with a heavy thud.

I cried.

Rhodes tsked. "I thought it would be more of a challenge."

With Topaz out, the barrier around the smaller witch's circle broke.

Ylena appeared.

Rhodes smiled at her. "Ylena, it's so good to see you."

Ylena, still in her crazed angel mode, stared at him with suspicion.

In in the span of seconds, a series of things happened: someone reached into my back, grabbed the dagger, ran it up my back, drawing blood, and threw it over my head.

I let out a cry as the dagger landed right in Rhodes's hand.

He closed his fist around the hilt and plunged it into Ylena's chest.

"No!" I shouted again, jerking against the angels holding me. I tried summoning my sword, my magic, but nothing would obey me. And the cut on my back began throbbing, which made it harder for me to focus.

Ylena gasped as Rhodes tested the dagger. He turned her back to normal, but he didn't stop there. He consumed her power, making her weak and frail. And all she could do was gasp.

He kept taking until she looked like a thousand-year-old mummy … and died.

With a deep inhale, Rhodes pulled the dagger out of her body, let it fall to the ground like crumpled paper, and glanced at me. "Your turn."

A groan echoed from behind me as Levi soared in an arc and flew toward Rhodes—his shoulder bleeding. The two grappled for a moment, and Levi's fingers closed around the dagger, but Sariel came from behind and sent a jolt of light magic directly into Levi's back.

He let out a roar and fell to his knees.

I called my magic. It fought and trembled against me, but I was able to hold on to it to send it toward the two angels holding me. It shocked them, making them release me.

I ran to Levi.

"To make sure you're not going anywhere," Rhodes said as he raised his hand and sent a big light bolt at me.

With a gasp, I banked to the right but wasn't fast enough. The bolt hit the left side of my chest with enough force to take my breath away and push me to the ground. I fell, my head swirling.

"Time to go," Sariel said to Rhodes.

He nodded. "The others will finish them off when they get here." He gripped the dagger. "We should get this out of here."

I watched with blurred sight as Rhodes pushed off his feet and took to the air. Sariel pushed too, but before she could fly,

Levi jumped at her, grabbed her wings, and drove her face first into the ground.

With a mighty roar, he ripped one of her wings off. Her horrifying shriek made me recoiled as blood splattered everywhere.

Levi started pulling the other wing.

Until a light bolt hit his arms and he hissed, releasing her. With trembling legs, Sariel pushed away from Levi. Two angels swooped down, grabbed her arms, and flew away with her.

Breathing hard, Levi sat back and watched as our enemies flew away.

With the dagger.

21

reached for me and helped me up.

"Are you all right?" he asked, looking me up and down.

I pressed a hand on my chest, where Rhodes's last strike had hit me. It had hurt like a bitch and I still could feel the aftereffect swirling inside me, as if he had let it slip into me to hurt me later.

"I'm fine." I glanced at his arm and back. "You're hurt."

He shook his head. "It's all superficial."

"We need to go," Rage declared as the rest of the angels perished at my friends' hands. He pointed to the sky. "The others are coming."

In the distance, a cloud of angels approached.

Shit.

Aspen opened a portal among us. We grabbed one another and crossed the portal. It took us to the front yard of a large three-story house at a cliff's edge in a thick forest.

We all collapsed on the soft grass as soon as the portal closed and we knew no one else would be following us.

The pain in my back and my chest screamed, but it was nothing compared to my wounded pride.

I had lost the dagger.

Rhodes had it. He had killed Ylena with it, and now he had it, and he was on his way to Elysium, where he would do angels knew what!

Levi reached for me and squeezed my hand. "Hey." I looked at him. "It's not your fault."

"Yes, it is," I muttered. "I was supposed to protect it, to keep it from them, to take it to a safe place."

Levi embraced me. We both groaned from our injuries, but we didn't care. Right now, I needed this. His warmth, his big, protective arms around me, his breath on my ear.

"We'll fix this, sweetheart," he whispered. "I know we will."

I held on to him, tight, suddenly afraid that he would be gone. He groaned, and I pulled back. The wound from the other day had opened during the battle and now a couple of thin lines of blood trailed down his side. It didn't look pretty, but he would survive.

"How's your back?" he asked, reaching for me again.

"It's fine," I lied. It wasn't fine at all. It hurt more by the second and I had a feeling that I wouldn't be able to take a step, but at the same time, I felt like I deserved this.

For losing the dagger.

The damn dagger.

By the light, if I let it, the guilt would consume me.

On my knees and hurting, I glanced around. Everyone was beaten, bruised, and bloodied.

To the side, Harvey tended to Ava's bleeding shoulder. Rage held on to his left arm as if it was either sprained or broken, Andre seemed to have a nasty wound on his head, and at the back of the group, Zad held a fainted Topaz in his arms, while Lacey tried to heal her in the rush.

A shudder rocked my body, followed by a sudden sob.

"I'm sorry," I whispered. A few of them looked at me. "For bringing you all out here and losing the dagger."

Abbie shook her head. "It's not your fault."

"We knew the risks," Farrah said with a small smile. "Besides, we'll get it back."

The others nodded. Even Lacey, who seemed focused on healing Topaz.

If the witch died now, I would never forgive myself.

"We will get the dagger back," Rage insisted. "But first, we need to regroup and rest." He stared at the house. "Where are we?"

"A warlock manor," Aspen said. His lip was busted, and his left eyebrow was bleeding.

"You mean, one of Soren's old hideouts," Wyatt asked, his tone flat.

I frowned. I had heard a lot about Soren, the first Warlock Lord. I had even been captured by some of his former warlocks months ago.

Aspen nodded. "Yes. But now it's one of the bases for our spy network."

At that, the front door of the house opened and two warlocks walked out.

"Aspen," one of them asked. "What's going on?"

"They are with me," Aspen said. "We were on an important mission, but it didn't go as planned. They need healing and a place to rest."

The warlock nodded. "Of course. Please come with us."

Everyone started following him with slow, painful steps.

Holding my hand, Levi stood and pulled me up. I gritted my teeth as a wave of pain traveled down my back and legs.

"Sweetheart, how bad is it?" Levi walked around me, and I didn't have the strength or the will to stop him.

Instead, I watched as the second warlock walked to the back of the group and knelt beside Lacey. They exchanged a few words. He then placed his hands on top of hers and they healed Topaz together. After a couple of seconds, the witch exhaled loudly.

Lacey and the warlock retreated their hands, said something else, and stood. Zad followed them, with a dazed Topaz still in his arms.

Approaching us, Lacey caught my eye. "She'll be fine," she assured me.

A sense of relief washed over me.

Until a finger touched my back and a wave of pain coursed through me. I almost screamed but was able to close my mouth and swallow it.

"You're not fine," Levi said, through gritted teeth.

"Look who's speaking." I turned and pointed to his waist. "I did a bad job there and it shows." I took a step closer and looked at him. "You're here," I whispered, suddenly aware that something had gone right. "You're back."

"Thanks to you, sweetheart." He took my hand in his and tugged me even closer. He leaned into me and rested his forehead on mine. "Really ... thank you."

"Oh, the almighty Leviathan said thank you about three times in the last hour. That's surely a record." I almost chuckled, but I was too busy enjoying this moment.

My chest started throbbing and I suppressed a groan.

Levi noticed, though. "Let's get you healed, sweetheart."

THE MANOR WAS EVEN BIGGER on the inside, going another two stories under the main floor. There was an entire infirmary with beds, all of them with curtains for division. Most of my friends and I ended up on those beds, waiting for the warlocks and Lacey to come around and heal us.

When Lacey stopped beside Levi, she could barely contain her tears. "Thank goodness you're okay." He hugged her, but didn't say much while she healed his injury, finally closing the cut properly. "I don't think I'll be able to erase all of it," she said, explaining that my stitching had definitely saved him, but it had also marked him in a way magic couldn't undo. "We can keep trying, though."

Levi shook his head. "It's fine. I like it." He looked at me.

Clearing her throat. "Right. Here." She shoved a black shirt at him. "From the warlocks."

Gingerly, Levi put on the shirt and I quietly mourned the loss of such an incredible view.

Lacey rounded my bed and stood behind me. She hovered her hand over my wound and started working. I first felt a sting, then warmth as her magic did its job.

"How's Topaz?" I asked. The witch was sleeping on the bed across the large room, and I could barely make out her form from here.

"She's fine," Lacey said, her voice tight. "She was hit pretty hard, but she'll be okay."

I bit down on my cheek, dying to ask her what was up between the two of them. I wanted to, and I would, I just wasn't sure this was the time and place.

Lacey pressed her hand to my back. "How does it feel?"

I groaned. "A little sore."

"That's expected, but the injury is gone. You'll be good as new in no time." She smiled at me, then turned to Ava, who was two beds from me.

I opened my mouth to tell her about the pain in my chest but shut it again. There was no visible wound, and right now, other people needed her more than I did.

I glanced around.

Rage was seated with Zad beside Topaz's bed, and his arm looked mended. Andre and Doreen were on the other side of Ava and Harvey, and they looked fine too.

Abbie, Farrah, and Wyatt were behind Levi's bed. The warlock who had helped Lacey with Topaz was now healing Wyatt's scratches. His name was Kadir, and he had been working with Keeran, the Warlock Lord, for a while. He and the other warlock, Bevan, who had welcomed us inside, oversaw this place, and kept Lord Keeran and Lord Drake informed of everything that was going on in their spy network.

When Kadir was done, he looked around and scratched his short beard. "I think everyone is healed now. The dining room should be prepared for you, and while you eat, I'll make sure your bedrooms are set." He gestured for us to get up. "Follow me, if you're ready."

Everyone got up and started going after him, but I stayed back. With slow steps, I approached Topaz's bed. Her skin was pale and she looked incredibly frail.

"Don't look so glum," she said, her voice thin.

I gaped at her. "You're awake."

She peeked at me with one eye. "Barely."

"I'm sorry."

"About?"

"Bringing mayhem to your doorstep."

"Oh, Ariella, we can try to hide from it, but as supernaturals, mayhem will always find us. I'm surprised it took so long."

"Still, it's my fault."

She opened both eyes. "It'll be okay. I'll be okay."

"But your agreement with the Mojave tribe. You weren't supposed to make a ruckus on their land."

"I'm good friends with their leaders and I'm sure I can make them look the other way. Don't worry about it. I'm not." She reached to me and patted the top of my hand. "Go with the others and let me rest now." She closed her eyes and whispered, "Everything will be fine."

With a sigh, I turned to leave and saw Levi had stayed by the door, waiting for me. As I approached him, he offered me his hand.

I stared at it for a second before taking it. This was new. Before, he wouldn't have held my hand while walking down a hallway.

"They went this way," he said, taking the lead.

As we walked, I glanced at him. There was so much to talk about, so much to understand, but now wasn't the right moment.

We found the others as they entered a room in the front area of the manor, near the foyer. We followed them into the dining room, with a long table for twenty.

Another warlock was there. "I'm Calder." He had cropped black hair, like a military buzz, and dark skin. "If you need anything, let me know."

He gestured for us to come to the table, which was brimming with food and drinks. We all sat down and dug in. After pouring myself some red wine, I looked around the table. Levi to my right, Lacey to his right, Abbie to my left, Zad to her left, Farrah and Wyatt right in front of me, and Rage, Ava, Harvey, Doreen, and Andre took the right side of the table.

We were just missing Topaz.

I took a sip of my wine. I owed Topaz a lot, and I would have to find a way to make it up to her.

Everyone ate and chatted with the people beside them, as if we were gathered here to celebrate.

After taking a few bites of my food—which was delicious—I couldn't take it anymore.

"We can't ignore what just happened," I said. The conversation around the table died out and everyone looked at me. "We got Levi back, and I thank you all for that." Levi reached under the table and placed his big hand on my thigh. "But I lost the dagger."

"*We* lost the dagger," Zad said. "We were all there. It was our responsibility."

My brows curled down. I could argue about this, but the guilt wouldn't go away, no matter what they said. "Rhodes has it, and while we're here eating, he's probably enacting the next step of their plan."

Rage lowered his fork and knife. "I agree we need to act fast, but we can't finish this with Rhodes exhausted and hungry."

"Or without a proper plan," Doreen said.

I nodded once. "All right, then let's come up with a proper plan."

"We're too angry and tired to think straight," Andre said. Even though he had been healed, dried blood caked his hairline, where he had been hit.

I looked around the table. We had all been healed and had cleaned some of the blood and dirt away with damp rags, but we still looked like we had been run over by tanks.

"I agree with Andre," Aspen said. "If we come up with a plan now, it'll be rushed and not well thought through."

I groaned, but didn't say anything. Not even Levi seemed to be on my side.

For a moment, disappointment cut through me. Before, I had kept to myself, not sharing my problems, because I knew no one would care about them like I would.

And now, that exact thing was happening.

Only it wasn't true. That was my anger—toward myself, toward this situation—talking.

Probably getting hints of my feelings through the bond, Levi took my hand in his and squeezed.

I let out a long breath. "All right. Let's rest. But tomorrow, we'll come up with a plan."

The others agreed.

"Right," Rage said. "We'll meet here before lunch?" He glanced at Aspen, as if to make sure that was okay.

Aspen nodded. "That works. And in the meantime, we can activate our network and find out if anyone has seen Archangel Rhodes since this afternoon."

"That would be great," Ava said. "Thank you."

The rest of the meal was quiet but tense. I didn't eat anymore, especially because the faint pain in my chest was giving me indigestion. Finally, everyone was done and Calder escorted us to our rooms.

Ava, Harvey, Doreen, and Andre shared a two-bunk bedroom, Abbie and Lacey got a room with a queen bed, Farrah and Wyatt got one with a king bed, and Zad and Rage scored a room with three twin beds.

Levi and I got a small room with a queen bed, similar to the other one.

"Not all bedrooms have bathrooms," Calder said. He

pointed to a door down the hallway. "That's the common bathroom for these rooms."

We thanked him and disappeared inside our bedrooms.

Once the door was closed, I leaned against it, closed my eyes, and exhaled loudly. I left everything behind the door—the dagger, the angels, the upcoming battle, the danger—

Everything except for one thing.

One person.

A demon.

22

I opened my eyes and found Levi three steps from me, standing right by the side of the bed, his gaze locked on mine.

"I don't know where to start," I said, my voice low. "Probably by saying I'm sorry."

His thick brows knotted. "For?"

"Ylena."

He shook his head. "She was the woman who birthed me, nothing else. She was an evil motherfucker who got what she deserved."

"That sounds so mean."

"But it's the truth."

I knew it was, but I was still conflicted, because even though Levi hadn't had any contact with her, I had. She had been my mentor, the person I had looked up to for so long, and she had turned out to be the worst of everyone.

The biggest enemy I had ever had.

And now she was gone and I didn't know how to feel.

"I know you're feeling bad, sweetheart," he said, his tone gentle. "She meant a lot to you."

"I don't think I would ever be able to forgive her, though," I confessed.

Levi nodded. "I know what you mean." His eyes narrowed. "Can you forgive me?"

"For?"

"The way I treated you when I was not myself. I remember everything, but at that time, it was like I wasn't in control."

"I know that. Why do you think I didn't give up on you?"

He erased the three steps between us. "Thank you, sweetheart."

I forced a big gasp. "Levi is thanking again. What in the world?"

One corner of his lips curled up. "I mean it."

I reached up and placed my hand over his chest, right above his heart. "I know. What I don't know is if you meant what you said right before you crossed that portal and left me alone at that inn."

He stared into my eyes, and I thought he didn't remember. But after a few agonizing seconds, he placed his hand over mine and said, "I meant it, sweetheart. This bond might have started with a spell, but I don't want it gone." With a growl, he pushed me back until I was caged between him and the door. He glued his body to mine and I sighed in satisfaction. "I want you now and forever."

Then his lips were on mine.

I was prepared for his hunger, for this kiss to be as crazed as the other times we had kissed, but instead, Levi molded his lips around mine and oh, so slowly, kissed me with something I could only think of as adoration, devotion. His mouth moved slow, and I matched his strides, but it was deep, as if he wanted to suck my soul into his. To imprint his lips on mine.

And I was all for that.

Heat bloomed in my chest and spread down to my belly as he pressed his body on mine, touching every possible inch. His delicious mouth, his hot hard figure pressing against mine, and his hard-on strategically placed low on my pelvis.

I moaned.

With a smirk, Levi broke the kiss and dragged his lips down my neck. "So sweet," he whispered before biting the sensitive spot between my neck and shoulder.

I wrapped my arms around his shoulders, grazing my nails across his shoulder blades. By the light, how I wanted that shirt off. All of this clothes off.

I tugged on his shirt. "Off. Now."

A soft chuckle came from him, but he didn't hesitate. He stood tall, his body still pressed against mine, and with his intense eyes on mine, he pulled his shirt off.

"Your turn," he said with a growl as he grabbed the hem of my shirt and practically ripped it off me.

Without breaking his stare, he reached behind me, unclasped my bra, and let it fall. Only then, he looked down and licked his lips, before returning his mouth to mine.

His kiss was once again slow and deep, drawing little gasps and moans from my throat. He wrapped his strong arms around me, pulling me even closer to him, squeezing my breasts to his naked chest. By the light, how I loved to feel his skin on mine.

On instinct, I wrapped my legs around him and then Levi was on the move.

He gently deposited me in bed but stood back to take my pants and underwear off. Then his. I squirmed, watching his glorious form, all corded muscle and a huge hard-on … I swallowed as he crawled over me, his gaze again locked on mine, shining with pure hunger.

Hunger for me.

Levi pressed his body down on me—oh, I loved his weight on me—and claimed my mouth once more. I wrapped my legs around him and pushed my heels on his round ass, placing his hips in line with mine, his length right at my entrance.

I exhaled a moan, in desperate need for him.

But Levi had another idea.

Still kissing me slowly, he lifted his body off mine and slid his hand between us. I gasped as his fingers rubbed at my clit and two of them slipped inside of me.

I cried against his mouth.

"Holy fuck, so wet," he whispered before deepening the kiss, if that was possible, and thrusting his fingers all the way inside me.

Heat already burned inside me, bringing in pure pleasure and lighting me on fire, but then he rubbed his thumb on my clit while moving his fingers in an agonizing rhythm.

I moaned and he swallowed it.

I didn't think I could take much more, but Levi didn't stop. He sped up his fingers, while rubbing harder against my clit and dragging his mouth down to my breasts. He licked the round swell of my right breast before moving to the left and flicking his tongue on my nipple.

I bucked against him.

His mouth, his fingers, the heat inside of me. It was damn too much and I wanted it all.

"Give in to me, sweetheart." He closed his mouth around my nipple and sucked hard.

And just like that, I broke. My body tremble as I climaxed. I was so lost on cloud nine, I barely saw Levi adjusting himself, but I certainly felt when he entered me, his length filling me up in a way nothing else could and bringing on another wave of tremors to my body.

He pushed until he couldn't go anymore and lowered his mouth to my ear. "You're so fucking delicious."

I wanted to reply, to say something, but my brain was mush, and my body was in flames. But before I could think of anything coherent to say, Levi closed his mouth around mine, returning to the slow and deep kiss.

I had loved his hungry and desperate kisses before, but I had to say, these were just as hot.

Slowly, Levi started moving. With a gasp, I clutched his shoulders, my nails sinking into his skin.

"Oh, by the light," I whispered.

"No, sweetheart, not the light." He pulled back a little to look at me, but he didn't stop moving. "By us. It's us, the way it's supposed to be. Just you and me. And we are so fucking good together."

So damn true.

My moans got lost in our kiss as Levi increased the speed of his movements, thrusting into me faster and faster, until we were back to the frantic, hungry rhythm of all the other times we had sex.

But this time, it felt different.

It was different.

This time, we weren't just sleeping together.

This time, we had accepted the bond, our feelings for each other.

This time, Levi and I were making love.

That thought, that knowledge, made me even more full of

desire, brought on more flames to my inside, boiled my blood with more need.

Need for him.

For Levi.

I never thought I would find someone, to want them more than I cared about myself, to not be able to imagine a single day without that person, but here we were. I had been without him, and light, did that hurt!

I locked my legs around his ass and lifted my hips, needing even more of him, all of him, now, tomorrow, forever.

"So damn good," I whispered against his mouth.

He bit down on my lip. "Damn right."

In one fluid motion, Levi jumped off the bed, grabbed my legs, dragged me to the edge, and then he was inside me again. Watching me, he hugged my legs as he pumped into me, even deeper than before.

I stared at him, at the pure pleasure stamped on his face, and damn, if that wasn't hot. Again, I adjusted my hips, giving him a better angle, and somehow, his length rubbed in a different way, hitting spots he hadn't before.

My eyes rolled inside my head as I swam in pleasure.

My stomach tightened and I knew I was close again.

"No, not yet, sweetheart," he said.

Gently, he pushed my legs to the side, making me turn to the right, and he leaned over me—still inside me. He pressed his chest on my left side and reached for a kiss, while he pumped inside me.

I gasped as once more, he touched and reached spots that he hadn't before.

"So fucking good," he groaned against my mouth. "We need to explore more positions, sweetheart, because if these are good, then I bet others will be just as good, if not better."

"Agreed," I rasped.

I grabbed his arm, pulling him as close as I could in this position. I moved my leg a little, angling my hips up, and damn ... so, so deep.

The flames ignited more and I couldn't contain them anymore. I cried as I came again, and after three more thrusts, Levi joined me on the other side with a loud groan.

Trembling, he lay behind me, his legs entangled in mine, his arms around my waist, and his mouth on my shoulder.

"That was ..." I started.

"I know." He pressed a kiss on my skin. "It really was."

The words came to my tongue. They were right there. I wanted to say them, and I would have meant them too ... but for some reason, I couldn't get them past my lips.

I opened my mouth to try to say them anyway and—

"We've had a long day. Hell, a long week." He rested his head on his arm, his mouth right at my nape. "Let's sleep, sweetheart."

For a brief second, I was disappointed.

But I internally shook myself. No, it was okay. What we had done proved our feelings. We didn't need words to make it real. Not yet, at least.

23

I ROLLED TO THE SIDE, A DISCOMFORT WITHIN ME, AND BUMPED into something.

No, not something. Someone.

My lips tugged into a smile as I glanced with sleepy eyes at Levi sleeping peacefully beside me. A warmth spread through my chest, pushing the discomfort away.

Turned to me, one arm tucked under his head, and the other stretched toward me, his hand on my shoulder, he looked nothing like a demon.

But who cared if he did? He was hot as hell as demon and he was mine.

The warmth became hotter with that thought.

Despite how we had started, how things went between us, Levi was mine.

And I was his.

He had made it clear that he didn't want this bond to end and neither did I.

We had chosen to stay together, to be each other's mates, even if in the beginning it had been fake.

I would accept Farrah's way of thinking and believe it had never been fake. No. Since its beginning, this bond was meant to be. That it had been fate working all along, putting us in each other's path and tying us in unexpected ways.

I liked that.

Right now, lying beside this man who had stolen my heart, I believed that.

Together, we could face whatever problems came our way.

I reached for him, but the heat within me became even stronger.

Dear light, we had done a lot not even ... how long had it been? I reached for my phone on the nightstand—it was four in the morning. Yeah, it had been several hours already. Maybe I could really be horny already.

I knew that if I pressed myself on him, if I jumped on him, he wouldn't stop me.

Emboldened, I scootched closer to him, rose to my elbows, swung my leg up, pushed him back so he was lying on his back, and straddled him.

Levi stirred as I placed my hands on his naked torso and leaned down to run my tongue on his neck.

A sound like a growl started in his throat, putting a smile on my lips.

"To what do I owe this pleasure?" he mumbled, his voice full of sleep. But as he said that his hands ran up my naked legs and my hips, showing me he was definitely awake.

"It seems I can't get enough of you." I bit the tip of his ear. "I might have to eat you up."

He chuckled, his body shaking with it. "I wouldn't mind that." One second, he was laughing, the next, he fisted my hair right at the base of my neck, pulled my mouth to his, and devoured me with a deep, hard kiss.

He rolled his hips, and I had proof that he definitely was fully awake.

I moaned into his mouth and he groaned. He broke the kiss and tugged at the shirt I had put on as my pajamas. "This. Off."

Smiling, I straightened and grabbed the hem of the shirt.

A sudden tightening closed around my chest and I paused. What the hell?

Levi rose on his elbows. "Sweetheart, everything okay?"

I tilted my head and waited, but the odd sensation loosened.

Shaking my head, I leaned into Levi and brushed my lips on his. "Yes. Everything is more than okay."

He kissed me back but lifted an eyebrow. "The shirt?"

"Right." I snorted and sat up again. I palmed the shirt's hem and started pulling it up when a swirl of pain bloomed in my chest. I gasped and let go of the shirt.

"Sweetheart?" Levi sat up fast and clasped my shoulders. "What is it?"

"I don't know." My voice broke as it was suddenly hard to breathe. The swirl increased in intensity and I gritted my teeth, swallowing a cry. "Something is wrong."

"I can tell. What's happening? Talk to me."

I stared at him as the pain increased and I bit down on my lips to keep from screaming and waking up the entire house. My head spun and my vision blurred, the world becoming a giant roller coaster.

Levi pushed me to the side and stood from the bed. "I'm calling Lacey."

"No," I rasped. I inhaled deeply, fighting whatever this shit was.

He paused. "Give me one reason not to?"

I shook my head, but that only made me dizzier. "I don't—"

Then the pain exploded within me, my breath caught, my vision went black.

And my heart stopped.

Sorry, not sorry? Continue reading Ariella's story with Wicked Angel, the fourth and final installment of the Rite World: Fallen Angel!

Get it from my Bookshop: https://julianahaygertbooks.com/products/wicked-angel

Get it on other retailers: https://books2read.com/wickedangel

THANK YOU

Thank you for reading *Fallen Demon*!

Reviews are very important for authors. If you liked my book, please consider leaving a review on my store, your favorite online retailer and/or on Goodreads and/or Bookbub, please!

Did you like this book? You can check out other books of mine:

The Night Calling (Rite World: Night Wolves book 1): she was abandoned by her mate, left in the hands of a terrible half-demon ... but now he's back and ready to claim her.

The Darkest Vampire (Rite World: Vampire Wars book 1): a witch releases a dark vampire from a curse, and becomes inadvertently bonded to him.

The Midnight Test (Rite World: Lightgrove Witches book 1): a clueless witch is invited to join a powerful coven—but only if she aces a difficult test.

The Demon Kiss (Rite World: Blackthorn Hunters

Academy book 1): a fast-paced story about a young woman who finds out she's a demon hunter, and the half-demon intent on protecting her against all evil.

The Vampire Heir (Rite World 1: Rite of the Vampire): a dark and mysterious paranormal romance about a vampire and a young woman with a secret.

The Warlock Lord (Rite World 4: Rite of the Warlock): a thrilling and kick-ass paranormal romance about a werewolf and warlock.

The Wolf Forsaken (Rite World 7: Rite of the Wolf): a heat-wrenching tale about a lost wolf shifter and a fae princess on the run.

Winter King (The Wyth Courts book 1): a fae king needs to sacrifice a pure-hearted human to save his kingdom from a terrible curse. Only, he soon finds out she's his fated mate.

Heart Seeker (The Fire Heart Chronicles book 1): an urban fantasy series about a young woman who finds herself at the center of a mysterious supernatural world.

Destiny Gift (The Everlast Series book 1): a post-apocalyptic urban fantasy series about a young woman with a special power that can save the world.

IF YOU WANT to see exclusive teasers, help me decide on covers, read excerpts, talk about books, etc, join my reader group on Facebook: Juliana's Club!

ABOUT THE AUTHOR

While USA Today Bestselling Author Juliana Haygert dreams of being a dark witch, a demon hunter, or a blood elf shadow priest, she settles for the less exciting—but equally gratifying —life as a wife, a mother, and an author. She resides in North Carolina and spends her days writing about kick-ass heroines and the heroes who drive them crazy.

For more information:
www.julianahaygert.com

facebook.com/julianahaygert

x.com/julianahaygert

instagram.com/juliana.haygert

goodreads.com/juliana_haygert

pinterest.com/julianahaygert

bookbub.com/authors/juliana-haygert

youtube.com/julianahaygert

tiktok.com/@julianahaygert

ALSO BY JULIANA HAYGERT

To find links and more info, go to:
www.julianahaygert.com/books/
www.julianahaygertbooks.com

Standalones
Daughter of Darkness

Rite World: Fallen Angel
Dark Wings (Book 1)
Light Magic (Book 2)
Fallen Demon (Book 3)
Wicked Angel (Book 4)

Rite World: Night Wolves
The Night Calling (Book 1)
The Night Burning (Book 2)
The Night Hunting (Book 3)
The Night Rising (Book 4)

Rite World: Vampire Wars
The Darkest Vampire (Book 1)
The Darkest Witch (Book 2)
The Darkest Magic (Book 3)

Rite World: Lightgrove Witches
The Midnight Test (Book 1)
The Midnight Spell (Book 2)
The Midnight Flame (Book 3)
The Midnight Secret (Book 4)
The Midnight Hunt (Book 5)
The Midnight Wish (Book 6)

Rite World: Blackthorn Hunters Academy
The Demon Kiss (Book 1)

The Hunter Secret (Book 2)
The Soul Bond (Book 3)
The Shadow Trials (Book 4)
The Infernal Curse (Book 5)

Rite World
The Vampire Heir (Book 1)
The Witch Queen (Book 2)
The Immortal Vow (Book 3)
The Warlock Lord (Book 4)
The Wolf Consort (Book 5)
The Crystal Rose (Book 6)
The Wolf Forsaken (Book 7)
The Fae Bound (Book 8)
The Blood Pact (Book 9)

The Wyth Courts
Winter King (Book 1)
Spring Warrior (Book 2)
Summer Prince (Book 3)
Autumn Rebel (Book 4)

The Fire Heart Chronicles
Heart Seeker (Book 1)
Flame Caster (Book 2)
Earth Shaker (Book 2.5)
Sorrow Bringer (Book 3)
Soul Wanderer (Book 4)
Fate Summoner (Book 5)
War Maiden (Book 6)

The Everlast Series
Destiny Gift (Book 1)
Soul Oath (Book 2)
Cup of Life (Book 3)
Everlasting Circle (Book 4)

Willow Harbor Series
Hunter's Revenge (Book 3)
Siren's Song (Book 5)

<u>*Breaking Series*</u>
Breaking Free (Book 1)
Breaking Away (Book 2)
Breaking Through (Book 3)
Breaking Down (Book 4)